A FESTSCHRIFT FOR BARRY COLE

All rights reserved. No part of this work covered by the copyright hereon may be reproduced or used in any means – graphic, electronic, or mechanical, including copying, recording, taping, or information storage and retrieval systems – without written permission of the publisher.

Printed by imprintdigital
Upton Pyne, Exeter
www.imprintdigital.net

Typeset by narrator
www.narrator.me.uk
info@narrator.me.uk
033 022 300 39

Published by Shoestring Press
19 Devonshire Avenue, Beeston, Nottingham, NG9 1BS
(0115) 925 1827
www.shoestringpress.co.uk

First published 2015
© Copyright: Individual contributing authors

The moral right of the authors have been asserted.

ISBN 978-1-910323-34-2

ACKNOWLEDGEMENTS

Grateful thanks to those who supplied photographic images used in the following pages: David Belbin, Victor Frankowski, Pauline Lucas, Kevin Milne, Maurice Rutherford for the letter reproduced on p. 72, Geoff Stear, and Adrian Taylor. Thanks, too, to narrator for their impeccable work. The editor wishes to thank above all Rita.

CONTENTS

Preface	1
Brief Biography of Barry Cole	2
Returning Customer	4
Michael Bartholomew-Biggs	
Bravo Books: a Brief Biography	6
David Belbin	
Barry Cole	9
Alan Brownjohn	
Barry Cole	12
David Buckman	
Cutting Back	14
Malcolm Carson	
Livre de Poche	15
Malcolm Carson	
Barry Cole: The Writer's New Life	16
Martin Dodsworth	
Dear Barry	30
Steve Hawes	
Posts from Mount Pleasant	35
Maurice Hindle	
Remembering Barry	41
John Lucas	
How to Translate Joy	58
Nancy Mattson	
Barry Cole in Beeston	60
J.S. McClelland	
The Uncommissioned Snapshot Shows You Well	61
Paul McLoughlin	
From "The Wind Dog"	63
Tom Paulin	
A Spirit of Place Neighbour	65
Barnaby Rogerson	
Letter from Maurice Rutherford	72
Half-Time	74
Hugh Shankland	

Naming the Animals	86
John Stokes	
Postcards in Code	94
Geoffrey Strachan	
Doodling with Words	96
Hugh Underhill	
There's Honey on the Moon Tonight	98
Hugh Underhill	
Broken Sonnets	100
In the Pram	101
V1s over SW!2	102
Nightingale Square RC School (1)	103
Nightingale Square RC School (2)	104
Nightingale Square RC School (3)	105
Nightingale Square RC School (4)	106
School Dinners, circa Winter 1946-7	107
Morgan	108
I Learn to Swim	109
Sandham and Gover	110
Olive Poupart, nee Ryder	111
The Coffee Cabin, Streatham High Street	112
My Mother's Death	113
The Last Poem	114
Check-List of Barry Cole's Writings	115
Contributors	117

PREFACE

This Festschrift has been compiled as a tribute to the writer, Barry Cole, who died at the age of 77 in 2014. It contains poems, fiction, and essays by some of his many friends and admirers, though there are inevitably absences. Among those who would certainly have wanted to contribute are George MacBeth, Peter Porter, and Vernon Scannell, all of whom admired Barry's work, both in verse and prose.

BRIEF BIOGRAPHY OF BARRY COLE

Born Woking, 13th November, 1936.

Moved at early age to Balham.

During war evacuated to mother's home county of Durham.

Post-war returned to London. Left school, 1952.

Worked as lawyer's clerk, then for Columbia Pictures.

1956-1958 National Service in RAF. Began to write poetry.

Following demobilisation worked as a clerk at St James's Hospital, London, then for Reuters, then Ledgers.

7th February 1959, at Finsbury Town Hall, married Rita Linihan.

At this time selling books by post, selling antiques from a stall in Camden Passage, and working some mornings in an antiques shop in the Passage.

Three daughters, Celia, 1959, Becky, 1960, Jessica, 1962.

1963 began working for COI.

By mid-60s poems were starting to appear in national newspapers and literary journals.

1970 appointed for two years as Northern Arts Fellow at Universities of Durham and Newcastle. Family moves from Gt Percy Street, London, to Hallgarth St., Durham.

1972 et seq. Returned from Durham to Gt Percy Street, then, later, to Myddelton Square. Succession of jobs, including flat-cleaning, assisting at the Covent Garden Book Shop, PPR Advertising Agency, temporary editor of *Nursing Weekly,* sorting office at Mount Pleasant Post Office, then, 1974, rejoined COI, where he stayed until retirement, June, 1995.

Died 26th June, 2014.

RETURNING CUSTOMER

Barry Cole often wrote about people (and ghosts) who walked his local
streets before him

I 'ad my first experience in 'ere.
The old man doorsteps us as we come home
and points up at our bedroom windows.

This Georgian street was full of seamen's lodgings
(so he tells us) while the docks were thriving;
our house called itself a "Men's Club".
But when The London Docks declined to "Docklands"
developers renewed the rented rooms
and then made good the bawdy-house.

So lawyers, academics and art-deco
experts now reside, in costly, compact
and pink-carpeted apartments,
where pimps and card-sharps used to hang around.
And there was ladies who would dance with you
or take you upstairs to their rooms.

His sea-legs, firm with muscle-memories
of ocean swell, made light of flights of steps
to learn that earth could move as well.

It moved the night a stick of bombs destroyed
the parish church behind us, then picked off
the nonconformists opposite.
The unexploded brothel was still there
to serve his generation: post-war sailors
wanting company and comforts.

I'm 'avin' one last look. He frowns as if
he can't remember who remembers what
or why he's found us here. We could be
strangers; some old ship-mate with his wife;
a bouncer and a barmaid from the old days;
or ghosts who haunt these premises.

Our Yorkstone doorstep is a fractured slab
of memory to stand on at the threshold
of experience he'll soon forget.

Michael Bartholomew-Biggs

BRAVO BOOKS: A BRIEF BIOGRAPHY

Bravo gave me my big break. Based on three chapters and a snappy synopsis, Hugh Chance commissioned me to complete my first novel. I spent the next year in LA, where I house-sat for an ex-pat producer.

In LA, I eked out my last kill fee and the small advance Bravo had paid me. One year became three. Hugh assured me there was no deadline: quality was all that counted. He gave me notes on the first chapters, pencilling out the over-abundance of alliteration. A year later, I sent the final draft. While waiting for Hugh's response, I did additional dialogue for the latest *Die Hard*, which funded my mortgage payments and paid for a business class flight back to Blighty.

In London, I rang Hugh. The line was disconnected. I didn't panic. Numbers change. I tried Directory Enquiries. They had no listing for Bravo Books. That's when I did start to worry.

Bravo Books was 150 years old, and some of its staff weren't much younger. The firm's literary reputation compensated for the paucity of their advances. I was thrilled to be with them, and certain that my big book about the north/south divide would find its true audience, unlike the unproduced screenplays I'd been so well paid for in the past.

But.

But Bravo Books had vanished off the face of the earth. I made a few phone calls. An agent's assistant filled me in. Bravo's parent company had been bought by Conglomerate A, who were chiefly known for selling cheap cutlery. They, in turn, had been bought out by conglomerate B, who were after the cutlery business. B sold off the books division to Publisher C, who wanted to add some credibility to its chick lit and soft porn list. At which point, all of Bravo's key personnel, including Hugh, took a redundancy package or early retirement.

Publisher C had been the subject of a hostile takeover. The book division ended up with Conglomerate D who wanted the profitable soft porn rights to make movies of the week for cable TV. Conglomerate D was later bought by multinational E, the online streaming giants, who had no idea that a historic literary publisher was concealed in the deal.

Where did that leave me? The assistant's assistant rang round. Bravo's other authors had found ways of getting out of their contracts. She suggested I tear mine up and look for a new publisher. My heart sank. I had touted my outline for five years before Bravo took me on. Few publishers would look at a novice who'd not see forty again. I needed to hold Bravo to its contract.

My producer buddy tracked down Sophia, an intimidatingly attractive, power dressed exec from multinational E. We scheduled a Skype conversation.

'You're a screen writer?' the Spanish babe asked.

'I've sold two scripts and done a dozen polishes.'

'Ever written for TV?' Sophia asked.

'I'm trying to stay away from that kind of thing.'

'Scratch my back, I scratch yours. A missing child thriller is all I need. Easy for a writer of your quality.'

Long story short. Sophia dug my screenplay. Conglomerate E had no interest in Bravo Books, she said. They would sell me the name and the backlist with working capital (in the form of money owed by bookshops) in exchange for four screenplays over three years. Not only was my novel to be published, I'd be writing films that got made. OK, the sort of stuff we used to call TV movies, but that kind of crap brings in decent residuals for years. Decades, if you're lucky.

Hugh was persuaded to come out of retirement to edit my novel. Bravo's Soho building had been sold off, but all of the company's files were in storage. Soon they had taken over most of the floor space in my London flat and I had a backlist ready to be digitised. The physical stock was in a warehouse, I never found out where. Hardly mattered, there were so few orders.

Although Bravo Books had been closed down for three years, few people had noticed. After the post office began to redirect the company's mail to me, manuscripts flooded in. I read the ones from people I'd heard of. Many of their novels were better than mine. Each had already been rejected by big publishers. Writing was no longer a career, I realised, it was a vocation at best, more often a hobby. Or therapy. Publishers no longer take time to build a writer's career. If a book doesn't sell, they get dumped. What was I getting myself into?

I wrote my screenplays and bought a couple of new novels to publish alongside mine. I kept my ownership of Bravo Books under wraps, so that my debut wouldn't be perceived as a vanity project. I paid a publicist to push out proofs to influential people. *Bravo Books is back!* our publicity yelled to people who hadn't noticed that the firm had gone away in the first place.

My reviews were good, though some pointed out my weakness for cliché. The print run, however, turned out to be ambitious. I was on my fourth screenplay for Sophia before I realised that 90% of my paper-back originals had been returned to the distributor. Our eBooks sold better, but brought in a pittance. By then, only a film deal would keep Bravo in the black. I flew to Spain with a bag full of books. Sophia said she didn't see a movie in any of the Bravo novels I showed her.

'The story of how I rescued one of the world's oldest publishers might make an offbeat biopic.'

'You're right,' she said. 'But it needs a bigger hook. What the story demands is a central romance.'

'It's always amazed me that a beautiful, talented woman like you is still single,' I said.

'I have started to regret putting my career first,' she admitted, a twinkle in her eye.

'Me too.'

Reader, I married her.

David Belbin

BARRY COLE

I'm reading the Birthdays column in the *Guardian*, always an antidote to the Obituaries. Suddenly my eye catches an adjacent memorial Announcement paying loving tribute to "COLE Barry", who had died one year ago on this day.

And at once I'm sharply aware again, of the gratitude I've long felt for Barry's books and for having had the privilege and the benefits of his friendship. As a talented and various writer and a very good man to have around the place (qualities which don't always combine) Barry was greatly appreciated, respected, and liked, within and beyond literary London at the turn of the 1970s.

Then the dreadful circumstances of his friend Bryan Johnson's suicide in November 1973 caused him to withdraw into the background as a writer – and while he remained known, he wrote very little in his long later years, which became a matter of sightings and citings for his friends and admirers. In the twenty – first century "Barry Cole was there" was well worth reporting when he was sighted at a literary event. And then, for a long time he was cited as an example of exceptional courage and endurance in resisting cancer – I quoted his magnificent survival to several afflicted friends. Quite often the films made by or involving B.S. Johnson would get a showing at the NFT or somewhere, and in *You're Human Like the Rest of Them* the young Barry could be sighted as a young teacher in the staff room near the beginning, catching an announcement of *The Archers* which is adapted to suggest the first use of the 'c' word on BBC radio. Sometimes an old copy of *London Consequences* would turn up – a fiction written by twenty London authors for a festival involving all the London boroughs (the idea was B.S. Johnson's) – and at the back you would spot the challenge to readers to guess which of the anonymously – written chapters was by Melvyn Bragg, Olivia Manning, Adrian Mitchell – or Barry Cole.

My own friendship with him was of the kind one never doubted, even when a meeting had not happened for years – so that doing a good turn at any time would be altogether natural. Did I know, Barry suddenly asked me, coming out of the audience at a poetry reading in a library in Kentish Town, that some copies of my last book had been unloaded at his local secondhand bookshop at a painfully reduced price? I was peeved and embarrassed about this, and welcoming the chance to recover them. "Shall I buy them for you?" he proposed. No one had ever made me a kind offer like this. "Well... Yes." I was impressed, and moved. The copies arrived in the mail two days later, and Barry would not take any payment.

Barry's own books greatly deserve to be taken down from the shelves and re-read. To take just one: In a novel like *The Search for Rita* Barry experiments in his own way with narrative, with a variety of disconcerting characters, even though he owes things like a zest for truthfulness in B.S. Johnson's fiction, sending his characters along real streets in a real London, having them mention real persons such as B.S. Johnson – and John Lucas.

By 2011 I imagined – having heard nothing from Barry or about him – that he might be too ill to venture out; but I sent an invitation to a September celebration of my own (July) eightieth birthday. To my surprise he and Rita came, for what was to be our last meeting, and a last, inadequate, opportunity to speak. We promised to be in touch again but after such occasions you never are. Or I was not. But I opened today my copy of Barry's 1973 volume of poems *Pathetic Fallacies* and there fell out the inscribed copy of his Shoestring Press Poemcard "Hands On" which he had sent me on 1st March 2012. He had thought of me. I've thought about him often since his death.

Alan Brownjohn

BARRY COLE

My first sight of Barry was of him in 1956 at Royal Air Force, Colerne. He was rushing duffle-coated for the London coach that would take him to London from midday Saturday to Sunday night on the weekly 36-hour pass. I was a shorthand typist in station headquarters and he a typist in some remote hut on the other side of the airfield, as it was a flying station. We probably became acquainted either in the cookhouse or the NAAFI. National Service ensured one mixed with all sorts and conditions of men and you soon found others with common interests. Barry, John Sansom – now a publisher of art books in Bristol – and I, among others, had literary leanings.

Barry was then writing poetry. I remember particularly a couple of lines of his: "O hat, O cat, O glorious bat/Come back to me, come back", reflecting remembrance of a childhood pet and love of cricket. There was a lot of ragging. Another line of Barry's: "I saw a woman passing on a bridge" prompted Sansom and me to send it to John O'London's Weekly's queries page, thus: "Dear Sir, can anyone identify the following lines from a contemporary poem, either "I saw a woman passing on a bridge" or "I passed a woman sawing on a bridge", which, when published prompted much mirth, if not, at first, from Barry.

Sansom and I were eventually moved to other RAF stations, but we kept in touch with Barry, married to Rita and living in Great Percy Street, Islington. Barry joined the staff of The Public Ledger, a long-published agricultural commodities journal, for a time became a spare-time bookseller, then eventually concentrated on his own writing. It was a time when little magazines were flourishing and he, Sansom and I started the pathetically underfunded Tantalus, a medley of articles, poetry and humour. Like all such publications it struggled to gain a sizeable readership. After an optimistic launch in 1963, it petered out in September 1964 after a four issues. However, it is ensured immortality in the British Library's vaults.

I visited Barry and Rita from time to time. Then when I joined the staff of a West End-based magazine in October 1964 they kindly put me up for a couple of weeks, recommending a lady in Highbury who had rooms to let. Thus I became an Islingtonian, which I remain. They had a growing family of daughters and I would occasionally baby-sit, grateful for the supper provided as part of the deal. It was at Great Percy Street that I met Barry's friends, including the novelist B S Johnson, poet and bookseller Bill Butler and master art forger Eric Hebborn. I recall Eric showing us a sheet of sensitive studies of babies' heads by Augustus John for only, I think, £90. *Really*, by Augustus John? – in view of Eric's later revelations, I sometimes wonder….

It was around the time that Barry published his first novel, *A Run Across the Island*, 1968, that our paths ceased to cross, although happily later they did again. Barry and Rita came to tea at the house where I now live, I would meet them at private views and a continuing aspect of life in recent years has been visits to Myddelton Square. There Barry and I would indulge in long literary and arty chats over cups of tea. These and he I continually greatly miss.

David Buckman

CUTTING BACK

Slugs have laced the hostas, and it's time
to lop perennials – lavender, catmint,
rusting rudbeckias – as though to garner
summer's recklessness into fodder
against uncharitable winter. But too soon,
for growth persists, new shoots in this
Indian summer. Give the butterflies,
the errant bee, a chance now the logs
are stacked and everything's in imminence.
Mulch the days with expectation,
not regret, for too much cutting back
can foil whatever may surprise:
the roses in the snow, the unexpected bud,
and, splendid on the listless ice plant,
Red Admiral filching what it can.

Malcolm Carson

LIVRE DE POCHE

We met around the record shop,
drawn by jazz as if on cue,
Karl-Heinz, Rob Stalk and others,
from exotic places then: Cologne,
Amsterdam, and Cleethorpes.
With jazz we held our own:
the endless hours of favourite tracks,
the lists of personnel, the greats we'd heard.
Yet it was the *Librairies*
that drew us most and those little books
economy-sized, functional,
their yen for subversion.
We'd ration our hours along the shelves,
the carousels, swap authors
we knew or ought to know,
ignore the glossier pretenders
not worthy of our shared confidence,
our new confederacy.

Malcolm Carson

BARRY COLE: THE WRITER'S NEW LIFE

Fifty years ago in London, going east from Euston, the potato market at Somers Town was still standing and the British Library unthought-of. The facade of St Pancras station was decaying unnoticed. A huddle of unconsidered buildings obscured the grandeur of King's Cross. But some things haven't changed. The Euston Road still comes to an end at King's Cross where the Gray's Inn Road bends south, and the Pentonville Road still takes you on up the hill eastwards to the Angel. Just as it starts its long climb, past where the King's Cross Odeon used to stand, and also the shop selling 'books and magazines' with its dusty display of doubtful novels, the King's Cross Road still branches off to the right, skirting the bottom of the hill on its way to the Mount Pleasant Post Office and Exmouth Market. They are both still just about recognizable despite the fact of change. As you get to Clerkenwell Magistrates Court, a building still in use in the sixties, but now a hotel, you can turn up the slope to Percy Circus, which is no Circus, but does have a blue plaque commemorating Lenin's brief stay in London. One side of the Circus disappeared in the bombing, I think; any way, there was, and is, in its stead Bevin Court, a great grey structure designed by Lubetkin and his colleagues, but nevertheless unpleasant to look on. In 1961 I could just see it from the windows of my room on the first floor of number 18A Great Percy Street. Generally I preferred not to see it.

I had arrived in London to start my first job, at Birkbeck College, a little over ten minutes walk away. The first-floor front room, which was mine, was a bit austere, heated with a paraffin stove, poorly carpeted, but with elegant windows and a high ceiling. Diana Furness, who had been at the Slade in the thirties, and who painted and wrote, leased 18A, the first and second floors of number 18, from the New River Company. Her paintings, careful, semi-abstract oils, were all about her part of the house; even the biscuit-tins in the shared kitchen were painted in a sort of Charleston style (she had worked for the Hogarth Press for a little while at the beginning of the war). You could say it was all a bit primitive – the bathroom was in a sort of penthouse over the porch, and the water was heated by a geyser. The room would fill up with steam immediately, the walls and sloping roof were so thin, and one took one's bath in the smell of burnt gas.

Down below, if you went to visit Barry and Rita through the front door on the left inside the tiny porch, the bath was in the basement kitchen, most of the time covered with a hinged table-top, as the back room in the basement also served as a dining-living-room. I found myself there often, probably on rather too many occasions, talking with Barry and Rita, surrounded by the three little girls. The style there was not Slade School nor was it Charleston, but number 18 emphatically had style – Barry's books in the front room, the little hallway papered with travel posters (invitations to visit unlikely countries, in those days given out free) and interesting *things,* Victorian or more recent, a bit of a jumble in fact, all over the place. This was the style of the sixties

Great Percy Street dates from around about the 1830s, quite a wide street, and nothing mean about the houses, though I doubt if it was ever a well-to-do street before the 1980s or later. Amwell Street at the top had a butcher's, a dairy and an off-licence, as well as the Church of England Primary School on the right as you went down to Rosebery Avenue. Up the street from where we lived you could walk through Cumberland Gardens to Lloyd Square, where the houses were only two storeys high but truly elegant in a Grecian style. Kevin Crossley-Holland lived there; the typewriter was generally rattling away as you passed by. I don't think I ever saw him in The Percy Arms, at the corner of the Gardens, but I was not there much myself, nor at Dirty Dick's, the other place nearby where Barry drank, in the street leading to Myddelton Square. None of this was posh, nor was it shabby genteel; it was just good style in an urban way. A lot of people were living there who had been there a long time, and you did speak to people in the street, just as, on a Saturday or Sunday, you went to market in Chapel Street, across the Pentonville Road, and saw them in the crowd. The market was in business all through the week, starting off as a few stalls on Monday and packed with them by the time Saturday arrived. Chapel Street was where you went for pie and mash – eels, of course: and on the King's Cross Road, there was a house that sold winkles from the front room on Sunday morning.

This part of London, a thriving, settled community in touch with its past but living in the present, was the heart of Barry's domain. Geoff Stear's good drawing for Barry's Keepsake Press poem of 1974, *The Rehousing of Scaffardi,* is based on the names of streets just on the other side of the Pentonville Road, and the poem's subject is

Keepsake Poem 17, The Rehousing of Scaffardi (Drawing by Geoff Stear)

gentrification, the process of which Barry recorded over the years in his journal. *The Search for Rita* used the street map of the area for its cover (Great Percy Street itself hidden by a giant pencil), and friends are referred to in the book itself. There is that very good story of the girl picked up at King's Cross Station in *The Giver*, which Barry could well have heard in The Percy Arms, though according to the novel it was in the Northumberland Arms in King's Cross Road, another cosy or not-so-cosy boozer, just at the bottom of Great Percy Street. Many of the poems start off or end up in the area – 'Incident in Chapel Market', 'On Strega's Several Lives', 'Punctuation', 'William Thomas Meredith, London EC1' ('Lived in our house in 1859').

This makes Barry a writer of and about the city, of course, but there is more to be said about it than that. The London in which Barry was a boy and where he went to school was not Finsbury and Islington but Balham, on the other side of the river, a place whose traces in the poetry and the novels are not so evident. 'I.M. Susan Hawkesworth' has memories of first love ('Nightingale Square; Endlesham Road, the green | commons'): but the essence of the poem is death and departure. Nightingale Square re-appears in 'Who' which has another negative ending: 'What I could not recall, and proved | the dream, was your age – or your name'. There is, too, the line in the Scaffardi poem about the place the old man was moved to: 'Brent or cosmopolitan Dagenham', replacing the original 'cosmopolitan Brent or dull Balham', (as it was in the Keepsake version). It seems an odd change, but meaningful. Perhaps Barry disliked 'dull' as the antithesis of 'cosmopolitan', which in the revised version is forcefully ironic at the expense of both Dagenham and the old man; perhaps 'dull' wasn't good enough to contain all he felt about Balham, the place where he failed the eleven plus, where his father led the whole family 'so long and dull [the word again!] a dance', where his parents, according to another poem, never called him 'son'. I think that the effective lack of an education, which Barry made up for by finely educating himself, and the defeat of not getting in to grammar school, especially galling for someone of such intelligence and sensibility, besides the pains of his own upbringing, made Balham a bit of London which he didn't want to lay claim to and could barely write about, though it was there in his mind all the time. His last poems, the *Broken Sonnets* of 2008, are all about Balham, but they are 'broken', that is, marked by ellipses and incompleteness, a clear statement of the impossibility for him of writing fully the memory of his childhood, but an impossibility looked directly in the face.

He made the Finsbury that he had settled in, married in, and brought his children up in, his own place. It was Rita's really, for she had been brought up round about Amwell Street and Myddelton Square. Barry's Finsbury and Islington stood for her and for what he owed her, but also for the new life he had made there after leaving Balham behind. I do not think it an exaggeration to talk about a New Life and an Old. *A Run Across the Island* looks back on the Old Life from the vantage point of the New; and there is a moment in the novel when its protagonist, Robert Haydon, is made to gaze through the window of the Great Percy Street house to see Barry in the act of writing about him. The scene represents the New Life as a writer's life, in a gesture which is celebratory, but only partly so. It also suggests, rather unnervingly, the Old Life prowling Barry's Finsbury, his chosen country of the heart, so that Great Percy Street stands not just for the refuge of a New Life but also for a refuge whose security is by no means guaranteed.

Perhaps it is not so surprising, then, that so much of what he wrote is concerned with matters of identity. What survived the Old Life, what the New one amounted to – these were abiding concerns. In this respect the novels are an extension of the work in poetry. I put it this way because I think the poems came first in significance for Barry and that he probably wrote poems before he started the novels, of which *The Search for Rita* seems the best because it is the most poetic and ambiguous.

Barry and I wouldn't have got to know each other if we'd not been neighbours. There was something unlikely about it. I was just down from Oxford, starting out on an academic and literary career, writing for Ian Hamilton's supposedly razor-sharp magazine, *the review,* and elsewhere too, convinced that the future of English literature depended on a rigorous sorting of the sheep from the goats. Barry read widely, but rigour was not a watchword. He didn't think in terms of 'literary culture' and the necessity of its being kept up; and in some ways he was right about this. The world has survived the disappearance of that idea, which at the time seemed, especially to academics like me, so vital. Barry, widely read and discriminating as he was, was not academic. Nor were most of his friends – Eric Hebborn and his partner Graham Smith, for example. Eric was an extremely gifted artist; I still covet a suite of his etchings which took as subject the world of professional wrestling, then in its tawdry decline. It was Eric's failure to establish himself as an artist in his own right that drove him to his successful career as a faker of antique drawings, or so some thought. Like Barry, he had left school early (he claimed to have set fire to his primary school), but he chose a different New Life from Barry's.

It was probably Barry's antiques stall that brought him into contact with Eric. I am not sure where he made his writing friends. It was, of course, a good time to be a writer in London. Crossley-Holland wasn't the only poet living living nearby; in Myddelton Square there was also Bryan Johnson, who was a drinking-companion, as Kevin was not. The Trigram Press, was just down the road before you got to King's Cross, publishing small editions of over-designed books of poetry, eventually including Barry's *Vanessa in the City*. There were little magazines everywhere, but chiefly at Indica on Southampton Row, among the revolutionary posters of tantric poses and 'Let him who is without sin jail the first Stone'. Barry had his own magazine for a while, *Tantalus*, in which I duly appeared, opining on the infant's sensations in the womb (Rita wondered where I got my information from). Barry was involved also with a magazine called *Extra Verse*, for which I wrote the introduction to a special number of Miles Burrows's poems – after his first book, *A Vulture's Egg*, he disappeared for years, but now is back from time to time in the *TLS* and elsewhere. I suspect it was through him that Barry met David (D. M.) Black, whose first book of poems, *The Educators*, had impressed me greatly. David later became a psychoanalyst, as did Miles, I believe. Literary life in London had many forms at that time, and was ready to go in many directions. I remember vividly the Sunday evening Peanuts Club, hot and sweaty, and operating close to Liverpool Street, where I went once or twice with Barry and Rita to hear him read his poems between sets of rather old-fashioned, whole-hearted jazz. There was a link with the Peace Pledge Union, and there were people there wearing its lapel badge, two hands breaking a rifle. It was a long way from the genteel atmosphere of Bernard Stone's Turret bookshop, which published Barry's first pamphlets.

In this rapidly changing scene, where Faber still dominated publishing in poetry but where the Beats were challenging the old ideas of writing for an audience, Barry was something of an enigma, a cool, unaligned writer. The same adjectives could have been applied to his person. For example, you couldn't play the favourite English game of 'placing' him by family and education. He hadn't been to Oxford, and I think he did tell me he'd left school early, but where had he been? I really had no idea. He said very little about his own past. His parents and family were never mentioned, and there was a sense of complete severance. Poems like 'You Can't Go Back', 'My Father Fathered Many Children', and 'Night Visit', to say nothing of the fantasies in *A Run Across the Island,* suggest, however, that Barry continued to try to understand his parents and their lives. His father was some sort of civil servant, but when I first knew Barry I got the impression, from his knowledge of antiques, that his parents dealt or had dealt in that sort of thing (it wasn't clear whether they were still alive, even). But then again, I was led to reflect, Barry could have picked it up when he was running his stall. At one point he gave me to understand he worked at the Baltic Exchange, something to do with journalism, but I hadn't the least idea what was involved. The Baltic Exchange should have dealt in timber and furs: would they have needed a press officer? Would newspapers have been interested? It didn't seem likely. In fact, the Baltic Exchange is a big thing in maritime transport, and what Barry was doing at the time, I think, was working for *The Public Ledger.* But is it my imagination at work on a bad memory, or did Barry deliberately set me up with his talk of the Baltic Exchange? Either is a possibility. If I've misremembered, I don't think it is just the familiar forgetting that comes with age; what I am remembering in my misremembering would be the sense of mystery about Barry, whether he cultivated it or not. He seemed to appear from nowhere, not just in my own life, but in the world at large.

Barry had a very particular way of speaking, clear, sometimes almost clipped, and in well-shaped, always grammatical sentences. There was nothing sloppy about it. And yet, whereas most people have voices that say a good deal about them, where they come from, but also what they are like, excitable or reflective or whatever, this wasn't the case with Barry. You felt he presented himself well in a voice that was his by choice, but there was a good deal in reserve that wasn't appearing. He was, of course, very striking to look at, the face wrinkled beyond belief for one of his age, the beard a statement in itself, and the clothes always changing, always stylish. He was a good subject for photographers, and his book-jackets show that they appreciated this (*Moonsearch, The Visitors, Pathetic Fallacies, A Run Across the Island*).

Goodness knows where the clothes came from – Carnaby Street in its very earliest incarnation, or whatever there was before that took off. Barry with his fantastic knowledge of London would have known where to go, and continued to do so all his life.

The mystery, the reserve, the dressing-to-kill, the self-determined identity – these are all reflected in Barry's poems. It is characteristic, for example, that many of his poems take the form of disturbing fantasies and parables. They are always guarded, never confiding (perhaps this is what he admired in Robert Graves's poems), but at the same time they are stylish, and stylish, I would say, in Barry's way:

> Hullo John is that you? Or is
> it someone else? No, it's me, you're
> right, it's me, what do you want me for?
>
> Want you for? Nothing. I just rang
> to find out how you are, whether
> you're moving or staying where you are …

> ('Person to Person')

Although the poem is called 'Person to Person' the idiosyncratic marks that would distinguish one person from the other are missing. The poem is a dialogue, but the reader has to allot the parts in it by working out what makes sense. The repetitions and the *basic* quality of the largely monosyllabic diction, however, suggest something counter to this work of dividing the dialogue appropriately; the two speakers have to be distinguished, and yet they feel interchangeable. The effect is produced with great economy in a poem of only twelve lines. This is Barry's style, and it can be deeply affecting, as in, for example, 'Melancholy':

> I am happy. I am
> not happy. I am not
> unhappy. I am un-
> happy. But I do not
>
> know what happiness is.

Again the 'basic' vocabulary and the requirement that the reader should make sense of the poem by applying logic to it. And again the uncertainty about what the point of the poem is, whether it is aimed at something about language (perhaps the shades of meaning in 'happy' which result from different grammatical possibilities) or at something about the person speaking (or writing: 'I am made of paper', he says later). Is the point a general one when the poet writes, later in the poem, 'I don't know what I am', or is it quite particular, about this poet creating this self on paper? There are further possibilities, of course, and the poem lets them be glimpsed, but only glimpsed, whilst pretending (if a poem can pretend) that what counts about unhappiness is the ability to carry it off with style. I mean to suggest an analogy with my sense of Barry's self-created personality, its reserve and its mystery, but not any kind of simple relationship. It ties in with a passage in his first novel:

> But why do I write all this down? You may as well get used to the question, because I shall ask it, or imply it, again. You, or some of you, will think this a novel; others an autobiography disguised as a novel; and others, fools, as autobiography.

According to the book-jacket of *A Run Across the Island*, the aim of the book was 'to present a true anatomy of alienation' – alienation was something we were all familiar with in the sixties, and it is reflected in the distance at which the reader is held by both the poems and the novels. At the same time, as the quoted passage shows, there is a contrary impulse at work, an engagement with the reader and a requirement that the reader should engage with what the writer has written. The coexistence of these two aspects is an important part of Barry's special quality as a writer.

The friendship between B. S. Johnson and Barry began when the former, who'd seen some of the poems, yelled out from a passing white van 'You're Barry Cole'. That was chance, but in a way it was inevitable also, and not just because Bryan lived so nearby. His fiction was self-conscious, alienated and engaged with the reader much as Barry's was. Both were interested in the truthfulness of fiction, in the often perplexing relationship between art and life. Both were ambitious and spread their ambition widely, Barry across fiction and verse, Bryan, more self-consciously modernist, extending further into film, where he had considerable success. He was known to be a coming thing, and reputed to drive a hard bargain with his publishers, standing up for the rights of the creative writer. He it was who organized a number of writers, including Alan Sillitoe, Zulfikar Ghose, Michael Moorcock and Barry himself, into a group offering to give readings and talks to whoever would pay. The brochure was, for those days, elaborate, and the photographs moody, though paying customers didn't emerge in numbers that could justify the publicity. What I believe was the launch party at 18 Great Percy Street was a good one.

Barry and Bryan drank together, and I did meet up, by appointment, with the two of them in the Percy Arms one night. The meeting was not a success. I had reviewed Bryan's *Poems* rather dismissively in *the review*, which cannot have endeared me to him – he did not lack *amour propre*. He was very late turning up, and not in a good mood, sullen and, I thought, demanding. Afterwards, neither of us sought the other out. He was a gifted man, and hard-working, busy with films, projects, and writing, incessantly concerned with the new, and I probably should have valued him more than I did. But I felt that, with him, ideas counted for more than the writing they were to inform. *Albert Angelo* builds up to the moment when the supposed author breaks through the wall of his own fiction to say that it's his own painful life he's writing about; *Trawl* is about that life vomited up as the trawler plumbs the uneasy deep for fish. These ideas, bold, obvious, and perhaps bold because obvious, needed more particularity, it seemed to me at the time, to root them in the fictions where they lodged. *House Mother Normal,* ingeniously and deliberately structured as it is, doesn't seem to me even now to realize successfully the voices of the geriatrics on whom the whole thing depends. The ambition is admirable, but I am still not persuaded that it is achieved. It may be that at some level Bryan himself was frustrated by the difference between conception and achievement in his work. The particularity of Barry's novels, by contrast, is one of the things that makes them still worth reading; the play between fiction and reality, which they incorporate as do Bryan Johnson's, is more involving because there is less of abstraction about them. Of this too Bryan might have been aware.

The end of the story in 1973 is well-known, but remains discomfitingly sad. Bryan killed himself, and arranged matters in such a way that Barry would break into the house and find him dead. Bryan, probably Barry's closest friend, the successful writer to whom he looked up, had drunk half a bottle of brandy and cut his wrists in the bath, the bottle left behind with a note: 'Barry: finish this'. Finish what? The bottle, of course, but what more did the legacy imply? Barry's life as a writer didn't end, but, since Methuen declined his next novel, and the firm was, in any case, well on the way to extinction, he became largely invisible, his great work his own journal, his poems few in number and not easy to find.

Beyond the horror of the scene of death, there was a different desolation. Bryan Johnson and Barry Cole were united by more than a common interest in experiment in writing, a common sense of alienation from the world, a common affection for the old London drinking places. They were both writers who had become writers *despite* childhoods that were difficult, marked by suffering and failure at school – state school, of course. This was what underlay Barry's New Life; it was his life as a writer, symbolised by Haydon's gazing through the Great Percy Street window. Johnson's death must have seemed to say that new lives of the kind that Barry had attempted weren't possible at all.

If Barry survived this terrible experience as a man and a writer, and he did, he owed an enormous debt to Rita and his children, and, beyond them to his circle of good friends. I am not qualified to write about that. But there was something iron about Barry's own character, reflected in the reserve he habitually maintained and in the way his level voice withheld further information than he intended at that moment to give out. There was a strength there that is very audible in his poetry, a strength that keeps him from saying too much, that keeps sentences from growing unwieldy, keeps complicated things simple, so that the reader has to get really involved with what is being said in order to understand at all:

> There are petals in my book, pressed
> flat between feint ruled lines of grey.
>
> None knows of these remnant flowers
> or of their long transmigration.
>
> I took them from an Italian
> garden, picked them from a warm sun.

And snapped them between my pages
until they dried like butterflies.

('Noted in Passing')

'Remnant ... transmigration ... butterflies ... ' – the longer words
are in conversation with one another, above the heads of the rest;
their conversation is about life and death and the myth or truth of
souls. It is up to the reader to hear this conversation or to miss it.
The poet – or the poem's speaker? – is an enabler in this, but not an
instructor. His strength lies in his ability to hold back from any
position of command.

The poem comes in *The Visitors,* the successor to *Moonsearch.* The
book has two epigraphs, both with some aptness here. The first is
from Corbière: '*Vous ne me direz mot: je ne répondrai rien ... | Et lors rien
ne pourra dédorer l'entretien* ('You will not say a word: I shall make no
reply ... And then nothing can dull the conversation's gold'), the
second from Donald Davie: 'The transcendental nature | Of poetry,
how I need it!'. 'Noted in Passing' is as silent as it could possibly be
about the *entretien doré* hidden within it, and its underlying motivation
is surely a longing for transcendence, even if that is not achieved. In
this poem, 'the detached pose of the observer' described on the jacket
of *Moonsearch,* exists alongside a concern for something that can break
through the distance between speaker and subject, speaker and reader.
Love is a word that appears surprisingly often in his novels as well as
the poems, and it signifies an emotion that might, should, or does,
transfigure the actual. It is part of Barry's strength that he never
betrayed his belief in such an emotion; he was obstinate about it, as
in the obstinacy with which he faced the 'companion soldiers' in 'How
I was hated'. They up-ended his bed every night; every night he
pretended to sleep on it:

Because I dislike them, they hate me,
tell me so. We hate your guts, Cole.

We hate the way you let us down
we hate your cowardice and reading.

Reading? Like reason, reading here
is confined to officers and their wives.

So every night they turn my bed, not
knowing why I have to lie on it.

The poem equivocates on lying, since it is a fiction that he really sleeps on the bed, but the equivocation implies the truth to his own nature that, by pretending to do so, he does not abandon, and that in life he did not. He made a new life for himself, and lived it through, survived what must have seemed like his own death as a writer (and therefore his own death – the title of the late book of poems, *Ghosts are People Too,* is about himself as well as other people). He was even able to write a poem (from the heart of *his* 'London, England' – called 'How Nothing Changes', and indeed nothing has changed in it:

What's your view on the world? Mine's
twelve panes of 19th century glass
dissecting ash and elm. Each is
twelve by twenty-two (this is London –
England). What I see is the effect of wind
upon leaves. But what have others seen?

The detritus of war, air of cordite, skid
marks of shrapnel. If I look,with steady
gaze, I can see your parents, hand in
hand, probably worried about money. Who you
represent is, of course, your decision. Still
the wind winds about, trees lose their leaves.

Nothing changes about wind among the leaves, except that wind is perpetual change. This knowledge of perpetual change makes it possible to see the war days in Myddelton Square, now a long time ago but part of the continuous process that doesn't change. The need for people to make up their minds about who they are or can be, is something else that doesn't change. 'Who you represent is, of course, your decision' – whether to perpetuate your parents and their worry about money or to be your own self. Just as in 'Noted in Passing', you are free to take or miss the point, which seems to be about your separateness from anyone else, but also about a steady gaze, something fixed, someone's determination, as it were to lie on the bed he has made for himself. There is nothing new about the trees losing their leaves, but there is something ambiguous about the use of 'Still', which suggests not only that the trees do this every winter but also that there is something reconciling in their doing so – reconciling 'me' to 'your decision', and 'me' to the facts of decline and death (mine and other peoples') – and more. I find in this a hint that the New Life had survived, with or without change; it was still there, and that Barry in his last years was true to his own gift. A remarkable man and writer, the one because the other.

Martin Dodsworth

DEAR BARRY,

27th June 2015

If this were a poem I would give it the title
'General Punctilio': but it is not a poem,
just the last in a succession of written exchanges that began
precisely 45 years ago,
a Saturday afternoon in Durham City
on the 27th of June 1970
when you gatecrashed my modest wedding party.

I say gatecrashed: how can you gatecrash a party in a pub?
Actually, you came with Hugh,
to quaff Mateus Rosé *à quasi-volonté*.
As the party ended, and my wife had changed her dress
for something *plutôt décolletée*,
you asked her name
and there and then penned two lines on a beer mat
as a wedding present:

'No dark sunspot can give such unrest
As the mole on my Patricia's breast.'

This is not, as I say, a poem,
but I can chop up my prose here and there
to echo what you once told me –
in your mock-paternal manner,
punctiliously using the end of a line
as your own kind of comma –
verse should be
a series of breaths.
Or, as I like to imagine it, Alec Guinness being Smiley
thinking aloud.

'Punctiliously', purposefully squeezed hereinabove like a hot and
                                                    swollen foot,
   shoehorned into an unyielding boot,

30

is a mere gambit, for which I apologize.
But punctiliousness is a quality in your writing:
observed in simple sentences, made up of short words,
except when long ones are to be rolled around our minds,
little, if any decoration, and a refusal of hyperbole.

The thing is, from the moment we met,
though I did my best to conceal it,
you became in my mind the model of how a writer should be
in verse, in prose – and person.
I should avoid the words 'father-figure'.
Fathers, when they figure in what you wrote
do not figure well.

"My father, at the time of his fourth marriage,"
says the narrator of your first novel in prose that, read aloud, reads
like verse,
"was a cheroot-smoking, crossword-solving, senior civil servant
nearing retirement…
I didn't like him. I disliked his shaving lotion, his loud voice, his
punctiliousness and the awkward backward tilt of his body."

"Punctilious", according to the sternly tautologous Shorter Oxford,
means "attentive to punctilios."
Near the end of the sixteenth century,
punctilios were, it seems, imported into English from Spanish *puntillos*,
plural diminutives *of punto*, to denote small points.
"I didn't like him," a small point, so much sharper than, "I hated him."

But there was a second meaning, acquired
around the Battle of Waterloo,
– how do they, the etymologists, know? –
by contamination from Latin *punctum*,
a process they, the etymologists
– as if to stifle doubters - call assimilation,
through which punctiliousness becomes petty formality.

In "School Dinners, circa 1946-47",
the seventh poem in *Broken Sonnets*,
you recall the cold, cold winter of your first year at secondary school
and your mother's anxiety:
"What was your dinner like? said my mother
… did you get enough? Are you hungry? …
Would you like a piece of bread and dripping?"
But the poem is foreshadowed by its deadly first line,
"Lunch, actually, said my father …"
Ah! *That* kind of punctiliousness!

Here he is again, in 'Learning to Swim',
From *Ghosts Are People Too*:

"This, said my father, at the Tooting baths
is the deep end. I looked at its green depths
wobbly waves distorting the deep white tiles.
And this, he said, is the shallow end (was

there scorn in his voice?) It, too, was green, but
close up, like a bathroom mirror. Of course I

jumped into the former, my fists banging
the chlorinated water, my legs flap-
flapping, all of me swimming for my life."

Twelve months after your father died you wrote, 'My Father
Fathered Many Children':

"I wonder if a leap year's long enough to give
a verdict or a judgment on your behaviour.
You'd argue continually (were you still alive)
that your manners matched that of any saviour…

I recall you sitting in your final car, dew
coursing your grey beard, and feeling – no, not pity –
but insufferable dislike (a quid pro quo too
pat, I know, to suffer without asperity.)"

You, Barry, were never *that* kind of punctilious,
not even on the page.
Instead, you end the poem with tears of regret
for companionship you should have had but never had:

"Poor dead dad – I was going to write 'old' and say
you swam from the Isle of Wight to the coast of France
and claim, belatedly, some sort of record –
why the hell did you lead us all so long and dull a dance?

I'm not complaining; may be complained against, no
doubt. But in your going there was no real dignity.
Here's a promise: when I give up, give in, let go,
I'll leave my children the other side of enmity."

And your children were always your companions, Barry,
indulgent, doting, yet respectful - to the very end,
they of you, you of them.

For, Barry, dear Barry, it was the man I observed
over forty-five years,
the husband, the father, as much as the poet – more –
who is the model I remember
con punctilio –
a perfect rhyme, you will concede, for
those hereinbelow.

Steve Hawes

Photograph by Victor Frankowski

POSTS FROM MOUNT PLEASANT

I have in front of me a small paperback, *The* INDEPENDENT *Coffee Book*, London, 2012 EDTn. The book is a guide to London's independent (i.e. non-corporate) coffee houses. Page 7 prints a striking photograph of a man seated at a table in the sun outside the coffeehouse *Caravan*, described in the guide as "a well stocked bar and gourmet restaurant." The man, who wears a panama hat and is engrossed in reading his newspaper, coffee-cup to hand, is not identified.

But for those who knew Barry Cole well – having to use the past-tense still feels to me like a forced technicality – the man cannot be anonymous. It captures his intense individuality, conveys something of his concentration, his self-possession and independence. Barry had told me of this photograph. He was pretty chuffed about it, as was his family. I asked for and was given a copy from behind the counter at *Caravan*. ("Friend of the author.") It appears in the present book by kind permission of the photographer, Victor Frankowski. Barry would have approved.

The bar/restaurant *Caravan* wasn't always so named. For years, indeed for as long as I can remember, the place was simply *Al's*. *Al's* was a bar which sold soft as well as alcoholic drinks, and it specialised in a great range of breakfasts, any of which could set you (me) up for the day. The excellent coffee was pre-the age of sleek Independent Branding. *Al's* stood at the southwest end and corner of Clerkenwell's Exmouth Market, diagonally opposite Mount Pleasant Post Office, and it was there that Barry and I regularly met in his later years, for coffee, catch-up, and, invariably, literary talk. The place was within short walking distance of Barry's capacious flat in Myddelton Square, whereas I had to take a bus from my flat north of the Angel, near where, in earlier years, Barry, his wife, Rita, and their three daughters, had lived.

Before we migrated to *Al's* Barry and I had tried other rendezvous. For a while we tried the small café which the Gazzano family opened inside their deli on the Farringdon Road, a little way down from Exmouth Market, but the café didn't work out, and so we decamped to *Brown's*. This was at Islington Green, half way between Barry's place and my own. But by early 2014 Barry found it too tiring to make the journey and we had to suspend our meetings. My last personal contact with him came in that June, when he sent a text message thanking me for passing on the kindly feelings expressed for him by my son, Matthew, with whom he had developed a warm relationship over recent years. He died soon afterwards.

Independence? Yes, indeed. Barry was all that Victor Frankowski's photograph implies, and more beside. He was special, a talented writer and omnivorous reader. It was partly the heterogeneity of his reading and his curiosity – not merely inquisitiveness, but, as older meanings of the word reveal, "scrupulousness" , "connoisseurship", and "nicety of construction" – which helped feed the way Barry's modernist impulse creates meaning and effects in his own writing. It was a kind of "making strange" process whereby his particular style of literary language emerged, whether moulded into verse or prose fiction. As John Lucas has written, it is Barry's status as "a very fine poet" that "accounts for much of his virtue as a writer of prose." Where I discuss his writing in what follows, it has felt right to confine myself to his major talent, poetry.

The making strange process occurs everywhere in Barry's *oeuvre*. Take, as an especially illustrative example, the weird mixture of deadpan observation, seeming nonchalance, and human concern at work in "Horsefly." This three-stanza poem is one of several about encounters with mysterious animality in the second section of Barry's first full collection, *Moonsearch*, encounters which, for all their apparent *sang-froid*, are not free of anxious consideration. The speaker of the poem notices the fly that "clings, hangs/To a lampshade", adding that "Of course I see him as a long/Legged horse, and watch him moving to/And fro."

Then, further consideration:

> I think, too, that I must
> Kill him; he disturbs my children.

The speaker strikes the fly and watches it

> Fall. He falls, and leaves behind him
> A pair of legs upon the bed.

That word "Fall" is emphatic, deliberately placed. Both the observant father's impulse to protect and the unsettling image of the pair of legs involve us in a domestic world where it feels as if some miniature tragedy has occurred.

Barry and I first met in the autumn of 1970. I had completed my first year at Durham University, having moved from Keele in order to study for a single honours degree in Anthropology. My main interest was in literature, but at Keele I discovered the subject of anthropology and, having chosen that as my specialist study, I was offered a place at Durham. I had by no means given up my literary interests but preferred to pursue these in my own way. At Durham I became involved with the university's poetry magazine, *Makaris*, to which I contributed poems, and I occasionally performed at poetry readings.

Barry meanwhile was settling into his Durham base, having been appointed Northern Arts Fellow in Literature for two years at Durham and Newcastle Universities. I think we first met soon after his inaugural lecture, though I recall little of what he had to say on that occasion. But soon we began to meet on a fairly regular basis in what became his local watering hole, the Victoria Inn – "The Vic" to locals – at the bottom of Hallgarth Street, on the other side of which and further up he had rented a house for Rita, Celia, Becky, and Jessica, and himself. By then I was in residence at Old Elvet, across the road from Durham Prison and about fifteen minutes' walk from the Vic.

My first visit to Barry's house came when he invited me to a party which he threw in order to make a wider variety of contacts than was possible through his official duties. On the way there I stopped off for a drink at what proved to be the sparsely-populated Vic and then, heading off for the Cole residence, I fell into talk with a man going in the same direction. In the two hundred yards between pub and house we found ourselves talking about Wittgenstein, I've no idea why, but the man, who gave his name as Peter Barham, proved to be a research student completing a PhD in psychology at Durham, and during my time in the city Peter and I became good friends, as, forty-five years later, we still are.

At that party I first met Rita and the girls, whom Barry on more than one occasion referred to as the Cole minors. The Cole minors were not, of course, allowed into the Vic, but Barry was soon entrenched as a regular there and many of our conversations took place between or over games of shove ha'penny at the bar – where there was a splendid mahogany board – or dominoes in one room or another. Barry was soon friendly with the proprietors, Betty, and her husband Joe (a guard at Durham prison), and he knew many of the other regulars, too. He was a popular figure. Since his main job was to assist and advise literature students at the two universities I would now and then show him some of my verse. He was mildly approving, at one point likening my comic verse to that of Stevie Smith and at another noticing a resemblance in my writing to John Berryman's idiosyncratic work.

I have an especially vivid memory of the time when Barry let me use his study and typewriter while he and the family were away on holiday. That was October, 1971, and John Lennon's *Imagine* album had just come out. Two years earlier I had conducted a lengthy interview with Lennon at his home in Weybridge, as a result of which the editors of a new north-east underground paper, *Muther Grumble*, asked me to review the album, a copy of which Apple had sent me on request. I felt it a great privilege to use Barry's hefty desk typewriter – an Adler – as opposed to my little portable, and to sit in the poet's Victorian chair, from which, feeling impressive, I could gaze from his great sash window onto Hallgarth Street. New to journalism, I was writing a music review at the desk of a man who'd published three novels and two collections of poetry, with a third on the way. (*Vanessa in the City*, which I later reviewed in *Palatinate*, the Durham university newspaper, of which I was then arts editor.) Here I was, perhaps on my way as a writer, but no more than a journeyman author, whereas, as a reviewer in *Stand* had rightly put it, Barry was "a fine poet – the real thing."

For proof of the rightness of this assessment I needed to look no further than the opening poem of *The Visitors*, which had appeared in 1970. "The Domestic World" begins

> Two feet above the ground, I cross
> half of Africa before breakfast.

What an opening! Twelve words to convey an image of the free-flowing experience of creativity that courses unbidden, bringing words and meaning together effortlessly in a nevertheless purposeful weave. The poem continues to image the writer's elevated state, logging the soaring flight of unassailability until, in the poem's closing lines, his necessary descent is recorded:

> All is equal here, I permit no
> ruffling of my life until, at
> night, my frozen feet return to earth.

Two aspects of this poem especially intrigue me, both of them intrinsic to Barry's style and concerns. First, there is the subject matter. The poem conveys, or perhaps bodies forth, what it is like to be "in the zone" of creative activity. (To borrow a term usually identified with sports commentators.) This is something Barry celebrated in the epigraph he put at the head of the collection:

> The transcendental nature
> Of poetry, how I need it!

The lines come from Donald Davie's "Or, Solitude," a poem to be found in *Events and Wisdoms* (1964), a collection Barry greatly admired, and he, too, needed that transcendence, as do many of us, as writers, but also as participating readers.

The other aspect of "The Domestic World" which intrigues me, and which is relevant to his art is the *place* in which he writes. This is identified in the last line of the first verse: "At night I spend some time at home."

But then the second verse again lifts off:

> This huge domesticity lets fall
> a pattern of proportioned events:
> the tea I spill no longer frets
> my temper and the failure of
> a friend to visit depresses
> nothing.

Barry preferred order to disorder, and above all valued the quality of life that the domesticity of home and family brought him. Here, the phrase "huge domesticity" gives us a clue as to how he works and controls his activity best at home, among physical and familial surroundings.

Perhaps it is because I can trace elements of transcendence and conjurings from his more quotidian encounters with various surfaces of the world in his final two collections, that I like these best of all. Both *Inside Outside: New and Selected Poems* (1997) and *Ghosts Are People Too* (2003) have front cover images closely connected to Barry's family. *Inside Outside* reproduces a delightful pen drawing by his daughter, Becky, which reminds me of work of hers I saw in Durham in the early 1970s. As for the photograph on the cover of *Ghosts Are People Too*: it's a photograph taken by Adrian Taylor, featuring his grandchildren Matilda, Lucas, and Rory, (progeny of Becky and her husband Adrian) together with Matilda's friend, Agathe, rendered in negative format. The effect is at once witty and haunting. The book itself is dedicated to Celia, Becky, and Jessica, the three of them by then assuredly Cole Major daughters. And by applying the inside/outside Cole vision in what are often sneakily effective ways, the poems themselves play joco-seriously with notions and depictions of mortality

I have other reasons for liking *Inside Outside*. In the first place, the book provides a wide and judicious selection of Barry's poems, which he chose in collaboration with his publisher and friend, John Lucas. Second, *Inside Outside* gives us any number of beneficially quirky and sometimes oblique insights into humankind, which, sharp as they were from 1967 on, in certain ways matured and deepened over the years. Besides, the copy of *Inside Outside* which Barry gave me on its publication has a special significance because of the author's inscription on the title page: *For Maurice – who knows more about these poems than most! Barry, 6 June, 1997.*

The "knowing" he attributes to me in that inscription I have always taken as a gesture toward saying that I shared many of the values he expressed in his poetry and in other ways, too. And so I treasure the proofs of *Moonsearch*, which he signed and gave to me in 1982, writing across the front of them in his Parker pen, "For Maurice – the second person to see this copy – after the publishers. Barry, retro. 1982 16 Nov."

During the time I was arts editor of *Palatinate*, I conducted an interview with Barry, which I am now unable to track down. I do, though, remember that among remarks he made and which I included in the text of the interview, was the existential pronouncement, "You are born alone, and you die alone." Are you? Do you? I do know that on the day Barry died he was surrounded by Rita and his family, all three generations of them. He may have died alone, but he wasn't alone. To echo a remark I coined in Durham and which caught Barry's fancy enough for him to repeat it on apt occasions over the years, it was a case of "an *oeuf* is an *oeuf*." That's my existential statement.

Maurice Hindle

REMEMBERING BARRY

I

We met for the first time in late August, 1966. He had been recommended to me by B.S. Johnson when, earlier that year, Johnson came to give a talk at Nottingham University, where I was then a young lecturer. After an hour spent haranguing his audience for knowing nothing about contemporary literature – an ignorance he took for granted – Johnson, perhaps surprised by my being able to quote one of his own poems, unbent sufficiently to accept my suggestion that we go for a drink. It wasn't politeness alone that prompted my suggestion. With the help of another lecturer in the English Department I'd just set up The Byron Press, and it seemed likely that Johnson, who was then poetry editor for *The Transatlantic Review*, might well know of some up-and-coming poet who would benefit from a first pamphlet publication. Yes, Johnson said, over companionable drinks in a city-centre pub – Johnson away from the lecture-hall was a very different person from the one who'd earlier brow-beaten his audience – a friend of his called Barry Cole was looking for a publisher. "And he's good?" "Why else would I mention him?" Johnson said. And he gave me Barry's address.

In the days following I tracked down some of Barry's poems to such places as *The Transatlantic Review*, *Ambit*, and the Oxford-based *Nine* (edited by the then undergraduate, Peter Jay), and wrote to tell him that I liked them very much and wondered whether he might consider publishing a pamphlet with the Byron Press. A typed letter came almost by return. He was grateful for my interest but had just agreed to pamphlet publication by Bernard Stone's Turret Press. However, it would be good to meet sometime when I was in London. (I had told him I'd be teaching for three weeks during the summer at London University's Victorian Studies Summer School.) As venue for our meeting he suggested a pub called "The Lord John Russell" on Marchmont Street, which was, he said, midway between where I would be staying in Cavendish Square and his own flat, off King's Cross Road.

At the agreed date and time I got to the pub, a single lengthy room which opened straight off the street. It was early evening and, looking about me, I could see only a few old women sitting alone at tables, in front of them glasses of what I took to be port and lemon. I bought a beer, found a seat, and only then became aware of a man about my own age standing at the far corner of the bar. He had neatly-cropped hair, a fringe beard but with a fuller tuft on his chin, was wearing a dark-blue pinstripe suit, white shirt and tie, and could have been a smart young business man. But what business man rolled his own cigarettes?

I went over to where the man stood, absorbedly tamping tobacco into a cigarette paper. His movements were leisurely, expert, and only when the cigarette was lit and I had watched the man's head jerk up and back to avoid rising smoke, did I ask, "Barry Cole?"

He stowed his tobacco tin into a jacket pocket, then, as though after a moment's thought, extended his right hand. A smile flickered and went, but what took my attention were his fingers, quite the longest I had ever seen.. Very recently – I am writing this at the end of August, 2015, forty-nine years almost to the day since Barry and I met – I heard Anne Stevenson recall that at her first meeting with Lee Harwood, whose July death had brought a crowd of us together in Brighton, she had been especially struck by the length of his fingers. Her words reminded me of Barry's fingers, reminded me, too, that some twenty years ago, in Sydney, the partner of the Anglo-Australian writer Michael Wilding told me that all writers have long fingers. No, they don't. Michael's fingers aren't particularly long. But Barry's certainly were.

"John Lucas," he said. He had a clipped, almost impersonal way of speaking, which as the evening wore on I noted was accentuated by the number of single-word sentences he used. "Impossible." "Absurd." "Quite". (Especially the last.)But he also spoke in sentences that rarely seemed anything other than fully shaped as they emerged from a wide-lipped mouth which sometimes, though not often, stretched still

42

wider in an expression that acted as a kind of half-mocking approximation of a smile.

I can't possibly remember all we talked about that evening, but I know we agreed that Donald Davie's *Events and Wisdoms*, published two years previously, was a good 'un, and we were united in huge admiration for Robert Graves. Afterwards, when I thought back to my first meeting with Barry, I realised that there was a recognisable Gravesian manner in the way he himself spoke. Anyone who has heard recordings of Graves reading or talking about his work will be aware of his disconcertingly odd, clipped, delivery, as though the words are being strained through clamped teeth, and how weirdly his mode of utterance seems to belie, even disown, the poems' eloquence. Graves reads his poems as though ashamed of his own linguistic and rhythmic richness, his mastery of "the singing line," which Michael Longley, one of Graves's ablest critics, singles out for especial praise. There was nothing remotely song-like in Graves's delivery of his poems.

Neither Barry's conversational voice, nor the way in which he read his poems, were as awkwardly reticent as Graves. He seemed to be entirely at ease with how he spoke. But the command of syntax, the sense of being in control, was very noticeable. When, after out initial meeting, I was searching about for a term to characterise this manner – not mannerism – I suddenly realised that the word I needed was "cool." It's a quality epitomised by the title poem of his first full collection, *Moonsearch*.

> "I am tired," says Selene, "of moving.
> And Endymion is a long time gone.
> Someone go and seek me out a King."

> "Tomorrow," she says, "I shall marry.
> I'll wear Courreges white at Caxton Hall.
> I shall cross the city ion a white taxi."

> II

> A seeker leaves to find her a King.
> "When he comes we shall marry at night.
> A Queen again, a beautiful Queen!"

"Poor Endymion," she muses, "gone so long!"
    Meanwhile, the seeker returns.
"Tell me his name," she cries, "tell me his name!"

"Madam," he sighs, his old head rolling,
"There is no King. There is no King."

The poem is managed with such insouciant panache, the rhymes so apparently casual, the break between parts so definite, that you could be forgiven for not noticing that it is a sonnet. But what are we to make of the way in which a Greek myth has been brought into contemporary London? Selene in Courreges white at Caxton Hall. Is this belittlement or enhancement? What does the poet think about it? What does he want *us* to think? But the poem's manner, its style, is an unyielding patina. It gives nothing away. It is supremely cool.

And it is followed in the collection by a poem called "Appearances", a tongue-in-cheek, witty tease:

You'd never know, looking at me
I had absorbed half a dozen
critiques of pure reason or had
made a list of the commas found
since nineteen hundred in poems
by Catullus; or had eaten
lychees in a town called Reading.

And you would not believe my talks
with Jack and Ho Chi Minh, and all
the subsequent correspondence;
that Marian Evans once ate
cornflakes from my daughter's dinner
plate; or the whole family lived
for a year in South Uist on tinned
rice; that my wife is the Goddess
Iduna. No – you'd never know
all this just by looking at me.

Of all the English poets who, following Thom Gunn's influential 1961 collection *My Sad Captains*, chose to write in syllabics, Barry is easily the best. In "Appearances", for example, he handles the eight syllable line without fuss and, by constantly pushing the syntax over line-endings, avoids any suggestion that the poem, as first appearances (ha! – to use one of his stylistic gimmicks) might suggest, could be in tetrameters. But for all the poem's teasingness, it is also serious. Appearances can work both ways. As disguise and implied revelation. "You'd never know".

II

After a couple of pints, Barry suggested we go back to his place for coffee. This turned out to be a basement flat on Great Percy Street, up from King's Cross Road. There, I met for the first time Rita – not Iduna, the Goddess of Spring who in Norse mythology guarded the apples that kept the Gods young, but an attractive, forthright mother of three very young daughters, with, I soon came to realise, a sharp wit and a sceptical wariness of literary – and other – pretensions.

While we drank coffee, Barry showed me drafts of poems he was working on, and it was some hours before I left to go back to my own temporary digs in Cavendish Square. But in the following weeks we met often, sometimes at "The Lord John Russell", sometimes at the flat in Great Percy Street, and by the time the Summer School came to an end we had formed a friendship that, with varying degrees of intensity, was to last until Barry's death in June, 2014.

In the early days of that friendship I found myself thinking, often, not merely about Barry's mode of speech but about his dress. Both seemed linked to the way he wrote, and at the same time both were forms of concealment. To put it differently: there were moments when I sensed that Barry's almost lapidary sentences were a deliberate acquirement. It was as though he feared he might not be as much in command as he wanted always to be. Speech and dress were forms of rehearsed control. But control over what?

He was deaf in his right ear, a condition brought about, he explained, during his national service days, when a piece of ordnance had without warning exploded near to where he stood. Yet for all this, Barry, like most writers I have known, was a good mimic. He could, and sometimes would, do varieties of cockney and West Indian patois, and for the latter in particular his voice seemed to drop an octave. Perhaps his way of speaking had about it an element of mimicry, a way of being a gentleman and at the same time letting you know it was all an act.

As for his laughter, it was customarily a mini-explosion of breath from pursed lips. And yet there were occasions when the laughter would become a bark, even a shout of glee, and then you realised he had deep lungs and, at a guess, was capable of projecting his voice, parade-ground style, over the squares and far, far away. I wasn't entirely surprised when I heard that in an earlier incarnation and before being beginning national service, he ran a skiffle group. Barry Cole and his Nutty Slackers, the group was called – "Nutty slack" was the term given to cheap coal mostly made up of dust, useful for "banking" a fire overnight – a witty enough title for a group which I've no reason to doubt was as rough and ready as most such groups were. Skiffle was the opposite of cool. It was dress-down, duffle-coat and polo-neck, do-it-yourself music.

I've no idea whether the Nutty Slackers were much in demand but I doubt they had access to a p.a. system. In those days most skiffle groups were acoustic only. But the Nutty Slackers wouldn't have needed a microphone, or even the megaphone with which some groups came ready supplied. Barry's voice would reach to all corners.

But as to his own, "natural" speaking voice, I was always in doubt. The poems, however, were full of clues, suggestions that his mode of utterance was something of a put-on, formed a protective barrier he chose to erect between himself and the world. (The Man of Mode is a kind of dandy, and "dandy" also means neat, trim, and, by implication, self-assured, self-contained.) But under the poems' almost icy calm you could glimpse a kind of anarchic energy, a dark gleam whose presence, though it rarely becomes craquelure to threaten a poem's cool surface, is there, rarely insistent, but never absent.

Barry was especially adroit at exploiting clichés. Perhaps there is a Cockney wit about this, I don't know. I do know that poems with titles such as "Love Me, Dog My Love," "Blind Date", and "Skeletons", have an edge to them which is sharpened by their punning titles, although "Skeletons" is, I regret to say, facile. "In a large blue cupboard behind my bed/ I have stacked a collection of crockery," it begins. And this is not all. "And ranging one side of the closet's length/is a perfect woman's effigy//…. Once a year I perform unspeakably bestial acts upon the silent effigy.// It is a cupboard of much interest/but I would never show it to my friends." The ten-syllable line is managed with Barry's usual aplomb, but given that the skeletons in his cupboard *are* being shown, the poem inevitably draws attention to a gothicry that feels more Hammer Horror than is good for it, and this is true of a number of other early poems.

But this isn't the case with "Ships That Get Pushed in the Night", which brilliantly touches on the cliché of Leviathon as the ship of state in order to voice a kind of underground protest at those who man the bridge – the ruling class, the establishment. Barry is not a political poet, but this poem has the sardonic force that goes with a disenchanted contempt for those who take entitlement for granted.

> There was this ten thousand ton ship
> leaning against the dock as if
> it were some impossible beast.
>
> We lined ourselves along the quay
> and pressed the bases of our palms
> on the iron of the starboard.
>
> The boat began to bang against
> the wharf and the captain left his
> wooden helm to investigate.
>
> "What goes on?" (he called through the fog)
> "Who pushes my ship, disturbs
> my landlocked equilibrium."
>
> "It is us!" we cried. "We push against
> your state and wish you a hundred
> thousand fathoms deep, we wish you dead."

Barry's last collection, *Ghosts Are People Too*, contains the characteristically understated but resonant "Renovation".

> Scaffolding encases the house; boards rib each floor.
> Windows, in a high summer, let in wintry light.
>
> It's a sort of armouring, a casing. Painters flit
> from floor to floor, white-suited brush monkeys.

It is difficult to write, read. Move to the back,
and they're still there; dabbing, scraping, filling.

It's as if the house had been rules, is governed not by
light and the prospect of trees, but by a Mondrian.

An interruption, a once-a-decade. This time, the front
door's been dressed in black, may well see us out.

I give in, discuss the progress, discover names, offer
tea, coffee. It won't be long, they say; it won't be long.

By the time this poem was written, Barry and Rita had long moved from Great Percy Street up to Myddelton Square, across from the one-time residence of B.S. Johnson. Johnson would I think have acknowledged the mordant, cool wit of the front door which, dressed in black, "may well see us out." "It won't be long, they say, it won't be long." Go back to "Moonsearch" and see how deftly, tellingly Barry can use repetition, there, as here, in this much later poem. It was a device he'd learnt from Graves: ("Despite the snow, despite the falling snow") though turned to very different ends.

III

Graves, it may be relevant to note, was in his early years a keen sportsman. Barry may have thought to emulate Graves in this regard. He was certainly by no means alone among writers in asserting or anyway implying a sporting prowess that invited a degree of scepticism. I think he did some boxing in National service but I'm less sure about other of his claims. On an occasion in the 1990s, when he and the writer and publisher David Tipton were on a mini-tour of the East Midlands and staying overnight at our house, Barry announced that he always did fifty press-ups before breakfast. David, a pugnacious character who was proud of his own physique, was taken aback. Fifty? *Always?* Yes, Barry said. *Always.* Without removing the cigarette from his mouth, David dropped to the floor, struggled as far as thirty-five increasingly agonising press-ups and then collapsed. When he had recovered his breath he threw out the inevitable challenge. "Now your turn."

"What, improve on thirty-five?" Barry, openly contemptuous, gave his explosive laugh. "Not worth my while," he said, and rolled another cigarette.

48

He also more than hinted that he was a better-than-average cricketer. Early on in our friendship he let it be known that he had played on a regular basis for Surrey Club and Ground. "Bowler? Batsman?" I asked. "Both," Barry said. And from then on he would allude to his all-round abilities as well as telling me that before marriage brought his cricketing days to a premature end he had turned out for some high level teams in the London area.

A pity he couldn't find time to play the occasional game, I suggested. Barry shrugged. "Not possible," he said. "Family."

Family didn't however prevent him from making frequent weekend visits to Nottingham. Sometimes Rita would be with him, but in the years when their daughters were small he more often came on his own. One weekend, which must, I think, have been during the summer of 1972, he was especially keen to visit. This was when he was still at Durham and putting together the collection of poems which would become *Pathetic Fallacies*. He wanted me to go over the poems with him. OK by me, I told him, but I was due to play cricket for the University Staff Club on Saturday, so perhaps it would be best if he travelled down in the late afternoon. But no, Barry would catch a morning train. "You're playing in Nottingham? Fine, there'll be time for a beer or two and then I can watch you play. I'll bring a book to read if I get bored."

Come Saturday morning, and as I was about to leave the house to collect him from Nottingham station, the club secretary phoned to say that one of our team had called in sick. "We need an eleventh-hour replacement. Any suggestions?"

"You're in luck," I said, and told him about Barry. "He'll need some gear, of course, and he's bound to be rusty, but he's a good cricketer. He'll be a more than adequate replacement."

I met Barry at the station. "Got you a game of cricket," I said. To my surprise, he appeared less than delighted by the news.

"I don't have the right clothes," he said.

"No need to worry about that. There'll be some kit for you. Well, shirt and boots." And I explained that the club kit-bag was always stuffed with a selection of different size boots. "Just in case."

After a beer at the pub behind the ground we walked across to the pavilion, Barry less than usually conversational. I introduced him to other members of the team, told them he was an experienced cricketer. Someone began rummaging around in the kitbag but Barry said he'd be alright as he was.

We lost the toss, our opponents, Woodthorpe, chose to bat, and Barry took the field along with the rest of us, wearing the clothes he had arrived in, even his jacket.

"Where would you like to field?" I asked.

Barry shrugged, indifferent. "Wherever," he said.

"Mid-on then."

Barry nodded and, having taken his tobacco tin from his jacket pocket, began to roll a cigarette

"It's over there."

"What is?"

"Mid on."

Barry wandered over to the position I'd indicated and lit up.

During the first over the ball was hit straight to him. Barry watched its approach with the mild distaste you might show for a foraging cockroach and, as it scuttled close, lifted a leg and let the ball pass underneath. Another fielder chased after the ball and lobbed it back to the bowler. Barry meanwhile concentrated on smoking his cigarette.

And so it went. If the ball came close to him he took avoiding action. If it passed either side of where he stood he simply ignored it. He was probably responsible for raising Woodthorpe's final score by some thirty or forty runs, though he appeared unaware of this, and, if aware, entirely indifferent.

After tea, which he had refused, our innings began. Recalling that on previous occasions Barry had mentioned a number of swashbuckling innings he'd played for Surrey Club and Ground, I asked him what number he would like to bat.

"Last," he said.

"Last? Really? But in that case you might not get an innings."

Barry shrugged. "Give the others a chance," he said.

As it happened, when the ninth wicket fell we were still eight runs short of overtaking Woodthorpe's total.

I had already strapped a pair of pads over Barry's cords. "Off you go," I said, handing him gloves and a bat .

He ignored the gloves, then, still in his jacket, walked out to the middle, bat carried over his shoulder like a gardening implement.

"Don't you want a guard?" the umpire asked him.

"Not particularly," Barry said. He lowered the bat, bent over it in a posture reminiscent of an angle bracket, the bowler ran up, delivered a straight full toss, Barry did not move his bat, the ball broke the wickets and Woodthorpe had won.

Later, as we were driving home, I suggested that he hadn't much enjoyed the game.

"No," he said.

He rolled himself a cigarette, lit it, and, as usual, jerked his head up and back while expelling smoke. "The cricket wasn't up to my standard," he said.

I glanced across at him. He was staring straight ahead, no flicker of expression disturbing the impassivity of his gaze.

IV

You never knew with Barry. He had a habit, or maybe a style, of straight-faced tale-telling which belongs to oral culture. I came across this style during several visits I paid to Australia in the closing years of the last century. It's there in a great story called "The Man Who Bowled Victor Trumper", in which two swagmen sit at a bar while one of them tells the other about implausible deeds he claims to be entirely true, including the one that gives the story its title. It's also there in a number of verse tales by the poet, Philip Hodgins (1959-1995), who for most of his short life farmed in rural Victoria, and whose "The Big Goanna" is a terrific piece of tall-tale spinning, or yarning. And it's the occasion of Les Murray's poem, "The Mitchells," where you can never be entirely sure of the truth of what either man who speaks in the poem tells the other.

> The first man, if asked, would say *I'm one of the Mitchells.*
> The other one would gaze for a while, dried leaves in his palm,
> and looking up with pain and subtle amusement,
>
> say *I'm one of the Mitchells.* Of the pair, one has been rich
> but never stopped wearing his oil-stained felt hat. Nearly everything
> they say is ritual. Sometimes the scene is an avenue.

Did this dead-pan style get transported with the convict ships that sailed to Australia in earlier times? I've no idea, but bearing in mind the Fat Boy in *The Pickwick Papers* and the Artful Dodger's fabrications, it seems at least possible. But then such tale-telling has always been an intrinsic part of oral or street culture.

There are poems of Barry's which hover between the truthful and the fanciful, and in which the tone is so level that you can't be sure *what* to believe. "How I came Through" begins, "My brain sewers broke/just after dark on Sunday", and though what follows is in some ways about experiencing and learning to cope with painful emotions, the narrative is conducted in a manner that won't countenance anything approaching self-pity, let alone a confessional form of utterance. Barry was contemptuous of the fashion for confessional verse which was all around during the 1960s, and he was especially scornful of Alvarez' claim that "poetry is a murderous art." The nearest he comes to the confessional is in a poem called "Depression", but although its last lines acknowledge that "The grey road's endless pit suggests/we cannot recover from what we live", both the generalising insistence (not "I" but "we") and the replacement of "where" by "what" deflect attention from the merely personal.

Even in "How I was Hated", a poem I take to be based on bullying he had to put up with during national service, and one where, Edward Lear-like, he opposes a mindless "they" to the loner, he ends with something closer to affirmation than dejection. "So every night they turn my bed, not/knowing why I have to lie on it." The bed he has made for himself is that of the poet, something of which "they" are ignorant. The note struck, is, in its way, reminiscent of one you hear in many of Norman Cameron's poems, a kind of witty, laconic acceptance of fate, although as far as I know Barry hadn't read Cameron, a poet Graves much admired. In "A Visit to the Dead" – a title Barry might well have envied – Cameron reports how "Long, I was caught up in their twilit strife./Almost they got me, almost had me weaned/From all my memory of life./But laughter supervened." You avoid whatever might be your fate by means of laughter which, at a guess, is as derisive as it is rueful. A comic grimace. The essence of the cool.

V

Fate is a portentous word, one Barry avoided. Yet it's worth saying that his entire lack of self-pity came in the face of what was sometimes a tough life. His father, who had been educated at Dulwich College but seems to have left the school under a cloud, did precious little to help any of his five children, and Barry, having failed his eleven plus exam, must have loathed having to attend secondary modern school, which he left without qualifications. From the age of fifteen until national service claimed him he worked as a lawyer's runner, then as a runner for Columbia Pictures, and after returning to civilian life he took a variety of jobs. These included working as a clerk at St. James's Hospital, London, followed by similar work for Reuters, then for Public Ledgers, and while doing his day job he began selling books by post; and on free weekdays he helped out in an antiques shop in Camden Passage, where at weekends he ran his own antiques stall. In other words, he worked very, very hard to make a living.

It's therefore pretty remarkable that he continued and even added to the self-imposed reading programme which he had begun during national service, or maybe earlier, as well as apprenticing himself to poetry. Most writers of his generation had a far easier start in life. They came from good schools, were university educated, and had no problem easing themselves into jobs that left them with long hours in which to practice their craft.

Barry had none of these advantages. But then, in 1963, he found employment with the Central Office of Information (COI) which guaranteed both a steady income and something like financial security. He was by now four years into marriage – he and Rita had married at Finsbury Town Hall on 7th February, 1959 –and had become the father of three daughters, Celia, Becky, and Jessica. And his writing career was beginning to take shape.

Success, when it came, came quickly. Poems began to appear in magazines and national newspapers, including *The Observer, Tribune, The New Statesman,* and *The Spectator. Blood Ties* was published in 1967, in November of that year he recorded some poems and an interview for the British Council, *Moonsearch* came out a year later, and at the same time his first novel, *A Run Across the Island,* was published in hard-back with a paperback edition soon to follow. All of these publications were given deservedly warm reviews and his name became, as they say, "current". Suddenly Barry was being asked to provide regular reviews for the weeklies, and he was increasingly invited to read to poetry societies and at some then newly-fashionable festivals; he began to get invitations to contribute to literary journals, he was even – or so I seem to remember – featured on the front cover of a fashion magazine. In 1969 he was included in Michael Horovitz' Penguin Anthology *The Children of Albion.* He had, you might say, "arrived."

It got still better. In the spring of 1970, the year of his second collection, *The Visitors,* and a year after the appearance of his second novel, *Joseph Winter's Patronage*, he applied for and was appointed to be Northern Arts Fellow at the Universities of Durham and Newcastle, a two-year posting during which he was expected to make himself available to students seeking advice about their writing as well as getting on with his own. Something of his time in the North is recorded by other contributors to the present book and I don't therefore want to say much about it, except that, having gladly written a letter of recommendation for Barry, and having been delighted when his application was successful, I was angered when I heard on the grape-vine that others who had backed Geoffrey Hill for the fellowship were out to cause trouble for Barry. Whether they did and, if so, whether he was aware of this, I don't know; I hope not.

In the period leading up to the family's departure for Durham ("Coles to Newcastle" was a back page headline in London's *Evening News*), Barry was in ebullient mood. He resigned from the COI. After his two year at Durham had come to an end, he was, he said, quite certain that he would be able to make his way as a freelance writer. Poems would always be at the centre of his literary life but the novels he planned to write would put bread on the table.

I was less certain. Both of his novels were good, both had been well reviewed, but neither had sold especially well. They were "literary" novels at a time when such writing was sought after or anyway tolerated by publishing houses who seemed to operate on very slender profit margins. The late 1960s was, no doubt about it, a heady time for writers. There were independent houses ready to take a chance on new novelists and poets, an abundance of independent bookshops where their books could (with luck) be sold. But as a great friend of mine says, "always remember 1849." The glory years couldn't last. Nor did they. The smaller publishing houses went out of business, the independent bookshops began to close their doors.

Barry certainly took writing fiction seriously. But there was an odd disjunction between what he read and what he wrote. *A Run Across the Island* is dedicated to Stanley Middleton, a novelist Barry greatly admired. Middleton is in the realist tradition. Barry not only admired Middleton, he was a devotee of the great nineteenth century novelists: Dickens and George Eliot were especial favourites, Elizabeth Gaskell only slightly less so, and he also read Trollope with pleasure. Arnold Bennett was another writer granted the Cole Seal of Approval and not merely because *Riceyman Steps* is set in the area of London round King's

Cross Road. When in 1974 I published a study of Arnold Bennett I dedicated it to Barry and Rita. The book picked up an appreciative review in the TLS although the reviewer did at one point wonder for whom it was intended. Barry wrote in to say that as it was dedicated to him and his wife he assumed the book was intended for them. This was witty but also made a serious point. Critical writing, Barry was suggesting, ought not to be reserved for an academic readership. He thought the same about novel writing. It ought not to be for a closeted elite. Hence his love for novelists of the realist tradition.

But *Joseph Winter's Patronage* apart, Barry's fiction isn't in this tradition. Far from it. The novels may be set in London, but their speculative, wide-ranging wit depends on allusion, much of it *recherché*, a clutch of near-private jokes, a stylistic range which makes much of pastiche, and a melange of narrative devices which, ingenious though they undoubtedly are, are hardly likely to guarantee a wide or even dependable readership. *The Search for Rita* was at best a *succes d'estime*. and *The Giver* wasn't even that. And with that fourth novel Barry's career as a published novelist came to an end.

VI

In the summer of 1972, Fellowship over, Barry and the family were back in London, and although they were able to resume life at Great Percy Street, Barry was now unemployed. For a while he worked for a Flat-Cleaning Agency (among the flats he cleaned was that of Suzy Kendall, a minor actor and sometime girlfriend of Dudley Moore.) Then he did time with the PPR Advertising Agency, after which he became editor of the short-lived *Nursing Weekly*, a more or less fly-by-night journal which lasted for as long as the *Nursing Times* was on strike, and for an issue of which I provided a detailed review of a book called *New Lamps for Old: A History of Nursing from the Crimean War to Now*. I remember that I rather took to task its author, J.S.McLelland, SRN, over perceived inadequacies in the chapter on Charcot, though I found in favour of a later discussion, "The Home Front: Nursing in England during the Second World War." The book existed only in my imagination, though I doubt anybody noticed.

When *Nursing Weekly* ended, Barry took work in the sorting room of Mount Pleasant Post Office, and was even measured for the postman's suit he would be required wear once he began life as a deliverer of the daily post. But it didn't come to that. In 1974, he was enabled to return to the COI, and he stayed there until his retirement in June, 1995.

VII

During the twenty-five years between the ending of his Fellowship and his retirement from the COI Barry published very little. His last collection with Methuen, *Pathetic Fallacies*, came out in 1973, the following year the Byron Press published a pamphlet, *Dedications*, and a few poems and pieces of prose appeared in journals. But then even these came to a halt.

Not that he had stopped writing. During this period he maintained his habit of keeping a daily journal, and he also wrote meticulous and highly entertaining accounts of the annual trips he and Rita took to Rome. At one point I was hoping to bring these together and publish them as a book to which Barry tentatively gave the title *Roman Candle*. But nothing came of it.

BS Johnson's death hit Barry hard. Johnson, who chose to kill himself on November 13th, Barry's birthday, also arranged for Barry to find his body. Some time later Barry wrote a very fine elegy for Johnson, "Odds Against", which was published in the journal *Ambit* and is included in *Inside Outside*. "Now tell the days before your death," it begins, and does so, in a manner which very remarkably balances affection, anger, understanding and generous regard for someone to whom Barry owed much, even if he exacted more:

> You arrogant, silly, benevolent man
> you bones before your time ....
>
> Awkward man! How you loved words and spoke
> of Beckett, claimed fame when broke
> and bought me crème de menthe
> in the 17th Arrondisement.
>
> You cracked old jokes at our expense
> would not admit that it made sense
> to put Austen, Eliot or Dickens
> some distance up towards the heavens.

You told me: "God's a rat and that's a fact."
That a poem should never be an artefact.
You thanked me, once, for caring for your wife.
Then ran a bath and took your life.

The separate sentences of the last four lines accentuate and intensify the previous stanzas in providing statements that cannot cohere. Johnson is presented in all his contradictorinesses. "Odds Against" is a poem which refuses to countenance, let alone indulge, the consolations of elegy. Its strained, near-broken music implies a truthfulness beyond conventional pieties or pity.

You could, I suppose, say that this refusal to go soft is evidence of Barry as the embodiment of the cool, and indeed I think it is. But for this to feel authentic the upholder of such a stance has to be beyond self-pity, and Barry was certainly free of that vice. I never once heard him complain about the way the literary world, so quick to adopt him, had proved equally quick to blank him out. He must have hoped that the publication of *Inside Outside* in 1997 would bring him renewed – and among younger readers new – recognition. But the book went virtually unnoticed as did the publication six years later of his final collection, the splendid *Ghosts Are People Too*; nor did the re-publication of *Joseph Winter's Patronage* bring him the attention he deserved. That novel, by the way, the nearest he ever came to mainstream fiction, has as dedication, "For BRYAN." Barry may not have intended that as a sly joke. But I wouldn't bet on it.

It would be wrong, though, to blame Johnson's death for Barry's waning star. It was one factor among several, but, to repeat, he didn't stop writing in 1973. The two late collections contain a sizeable number of good new poems. That they were hardly reviewed tells us much more about the limitations of journal editors than it does about the durability of Barry's work.

John Lucas

HOW TO TRANSLATE JOY

Barry Cole loved Italy, so here's a poem made of words found
on page 135 of The Collins Paperback Italian Dictionary.

Here we are at the knee page, the jeweller's page,
indeed, it's a page of joy, so let's juggle words
for joy is the root of all jewellery.

Do not sneer: all the toys are skittish here
for this is a page of greed and gambling,
indeed, since yesterday everything's at stake.

We can while away the hours leafing through
this Japanese garden, count irises and hyacinths
or sleep like dormice until the fiddlers arrive.

Here the javelin-throwers are greedy for thrills,
jolly for gin, comical as journalists
in Jordan who never can speak-it the lingoese.

Already they are sinking under yellow paper,
jiggling their knees like jelly babies,
throwing away their careers-o.

Here the newsagent grows junipers in jars,
shuffles melds and games of gin rummy,
gambles for knick-knacks in jade.

Here the gymnast goes to grammar school,
the jaguar springs from cage to kindergarten,
the fiddler bangs his knee on a broomstick.

None of this is cast in iron:
there's no such thing
as a gynaecological joke.

A garland of yellow lilies
is better than a jeweller's jacket
or a juggler's waistcoat.

A tasty morsel for a jaguar
is gluttony for a dormouse,
so let us fiddle away our time,

dandle our sweethearts
on our knees, sing every ditty
in Berlusconi's dictionary.

Nancy Mattson

BARRY COLE IN BEESTON

Beeston is one of Nottingham's satellite towns, a province of the Provinces. Barry and Rita used to come quite often to stay with our friends, the Lucases, who lived just across the road from us. Barry affected a metropolitan hauteur when in Beeston, which he called Beastly. Beeston has good pubs, and in them Barry liked to impress the locals. He did this partly by his dress, which seemed to be modelled on the young Disraeli, and partly by voicing strong opinions in a voice which was a little too loud.

Barry's opinions were hard to pin down to a system. When talking from the top down, about national and international affairs, he would sound like a church and king Tory, but when talking from the bottom up, about the lives some people were forced to live, he sounded left-wing Labour. Barry never forgot he had been an underdog, and he always defended underdogs when he felt he had to. He was very shrewd, even prescient. He was the first person I ever heard say clearly that limp-wristed western European humanitarianism would find it hard to resist the sharp edges of Islam.

I'm sure Barry enjoyed strutting his hour in Beeston, one exotic among everyday people. I was always sorry to see him go, and was left with the feeling that we had been touched by something out of the ordinary. I shall miss him.

J.S. McClelland

THE UNCOMMISSIONED SNAPSHOT SHOWS
YOU WELL

for, in retrospect, Barry Cole

When Fr. Gilligan found our class
without a teacher he found me
with an NME that I could get rid of
for a start spread out before me
on my front-row desk. It was there
still when he returned to say someone
was on his way and I was to wait
outside the staffroom where I protested
having shoes on my feet didn't mean
I was walking. I got off lightly,
though the devil pushed me
lurching down the stairs.

No one asked if you minded being snapped
with a paper spread out before you
at an outside table with a sturdy cup.
The brim of your panama slants down
towards the page like a frisbie, your hands
gripping the *Evening Standard* or the *LRB*
(to Gilligan it would have mattered which)
against a sudden breeze or in disgust
at what there is to read, your elbows hinged
under your nose on the table's edge. Someone
obviously thought this an excellent shot,
used it to advertise the place. That hat

went everywhere. How nearly I wore mine
to see you off. I should've done. Of course,
you might not have been reading at all,
but trying to outstare your antimuse,
your eyes polishing your unbrushed shoes.
I doubt it, though. Reading is collecting

stuff to remake into poetry, to mine
for the proper sense you'd make of it,
and you'd need to be on your own for that,
with a sip of whatever the time of day
invites, though walking and observing,
which you also did, would also do.

Paul McLoughlin

FROM "THE WIND DOG"

while I'm out after mackerel
in an open boat
– blue blue sky
after a skift of rain
the wet wondrous sky
stretched tight like a bubble

– hey Tammie Jack says
d'you see thon wind dog?
look yonder
– what's a wind dog captain?
– ack a wee broken bitta rainbow
tha's a wind dog

we were neither off Coney Island
nor floating down Cypress
Avenoo
– we were out
in the Gweebarra Bay
so I say to myself *Gweebarra*
and drive westward
leaving the picky saltminers
of Carrickfergus behind
me and that lover
of women and Donegal
– "ack Louis poor Louis!"
was all Hammond's aunt the bishop's
housekeeper could say at the end
it was too looey late to tape her
she was too far gone
what with age and with drink
hardly a mile to go
before she shleeps
hardly a mile to go
before she shleeps
– there used to be such crack in that kitchen

her and the maid
always laughing and yarning the pair of them
and wee Louis in the room above
hearing the brangle of talk
rising through the floorboards

o chitterin chatterin platinum licht
the bow shall be in the clouds
and I will look upon it
to remember the everlasting testament
between God and all that liveth upon earth
whatsoever flesh or faith it be
– they may have turned Tyndale into tinder
but the bow he wrought lives high
in this wet blue sky

Tom Paulin

A SPIRIT OF PLACE NEIGHBOUR

We came to live in Islington twenty years ago, moving east from Maida Vale. It had been a perfect base for two young travel-writers to write guide-books from, plot film scripts and entertain. Our sitting room-attic was lined with mattresses and cushions which could become beds at the drop of a backpack. But when we moved east, we were also leaving the over-entitled world of West London for a living neighbourhood which had schools, pubs, cafes and shops that you could push a pram too. Having spent years exploring the city centres of North Africa, Turkey, Russia and the Middle East, and identifying the most intriguing places to stay, we also wanted to find something that was charged with some history and character in our own city.

An artist, Hugo Grenville, had first shown us just how beautiful parts of south Islington could be, when we came and shared a picnic with him while he painted a terrace of houses that rippled down the hill of Amwell Street. The house that we bought is close to where he had set up his easel that day. We both fell in love with the mood of our house the moment we walked through its battered door. From our bedroom window you could look at a noisy corner pub in one direction (then packed with Irish musicians with Feinian loyalties that included the young Pete Docherty) and a Regency version of a Gothic church in the other (run by a charming, gay, incense-scented, High-Church vicar). The owner adored his freehold house and had spent years unpicking the layers of paint and restoring the plaster-work by hand. He had also created a vast map of London, copied from a 1745 etching, which filled the hall. This he left to us as a gift, alongside a fresh bar of soap on the basin. He had also invited us to his leaving party so that we could meet our new neighbours. We came and shook hands, but decided not to stay too long. We did not want to ruin his evening by looking too eagerly possessive. He had to sell in order to be closer to his engineering business in the Midlands, but was also clearly sad to be selling this sliver of a London terrace.

But it was a considerate thing to have done. Once we moved in, various neighbours felt free to reintroduce themselves. One of the oddest of these was a man who lived just around the corner, in a flat which allowed him to overlook the gardens of Myddleton Square from his desk at the window. He was a published poet and a novelist with a beard and a full head of grey unkempt hair that framed a crinkly parchment face, lined with the sort of Auden creases that you only earn from a lifetime of devoted smoking. His name was Barry Cole, and later I would identify many of his London-incubated poems in anthologies before gradually acquiring his back list. He customarily wore a grey hat and had fine hands that were seldom seen without either a cigarette, a pen or a paper in them. At the time we first met he was tutoring a young neighbour through his English A level. I think this young man, like myself, had been expelled from his boarding school. I liked Barry the moment we first talked, for he happily confessed that there was very little that he could teach this bright, questing mind, but that he liked the conspiratorial way he was paid cash by the father and that all writers benefit from the discipline of a schedule and an editorial blue pen.

Barry was always a distinctive figure on the street, for he never appeared to be in hurry, but always had a sense of purpose. He never seemed to be looking about him, but I soon learnt that he was absorbing every nuance of the streets around him. I found out that he knew every story of every shop in the neighbourhood, chronicled not as a gossip, but with a magisterial detachment, as if he was a geologist observing the layers of the past. He had the soul of a cat, not of a dog. He was almost always alone, and never the first to offer a greeting or make eye contact, but delighted to engage in talk when accosted. He also had good manners, never looked over your shoulder or glanced at his watch, but always gave you the dignity of his attention. Our meetings were always accidental, but they were frequent for Barry Cole, like myself, loved to cut up his day with seemingly purposeful walks, which actually led towards a café. We were both afficionados of independent, family-run businesses which took their coffee seriously. We also both liked to make use of the quiet, mid-morning pause in business after the flurry of breakfast meetings had finished, as well as the other, three o'clock, slump in their daily trade. At those moments you could spread your papers on the table around you, work your way through the TLS or work on some proofs. If you work at home, most especially if you are a writer, it is useful to shake some fresh thoughts into your head by walking, and it is vital for our sanity to be observed and acknowledged, even if it is only in the rituals of counting out your change. By moving between cafés, we remained regulars but not habitués and hid from any particular establishment just how much of our week was spent as flaneurs, walking and

stopping and reading. But walking towards a distant table is work. It allows the different halves of the brain to swop over the levers of control, so the assertive, risk-taking, creative self can be replaced by the calmer, rule-abiding editorial side.

I found out that Barry was very alive to these two internal roles. As a poet, he had long accustomed himself to transmuting emotion into language in some volcanic internal forge and then patiently fine-chiseling this language down to its core. I remember his disdain for some free verse that I was once admiring, which he (following Robert Frost) likened to playing tennis without lines or cricket without a wicket. He was certainly an immaculate editor, and for decades (once we set up as publishers) we employed him to proofread, which he did with precision. Indeed sometimes he would do it unaided, and unpaid, to an article of mine, especially after it had been published. It was always useful to see how much more work can be done to a piece of writing, and I think it amused him to see how slack the various sub-editors of national broadsheets had become, not to mention myself.

He was a fine and precise reader, crisscrossing the various papers that he approved of, and in his heyday there was seldom a fortnight in which he did not post a clipping through our letter box with an annotation, or some notice that I had missed, some writer that we had talked about, or something to do with early Islam, which he knew I was working on. He also approved of what we were doing in the way of a business, which was to revive forgotten travel writers and reissue their works in smart new editions with freshly designed type. But I also remember the day when my wife, who is in charge of all Editorial matters in our small publishing house, realized that Barry had lost his immaculate gift for proofing. It was after his first and very successful treatment for his cancer, where the doctors managed to give him another eight years of vigorous life. At about the same time, he told me that being cured of cancer had unblocked years of poetic reticence, and that he had never felt so certain of his voice or so thrilled to be writing. I liked that, and was amused that the very powerful and concise editor within him had been eclipsed by this surge of creativity.

Years before he had already told me, without a flicker of embarrassment or a whimper of self-pity, about his relationship with alcohol. I think it had been the theatre for some of his most important early literary friendships (most especially with the charismatic B.S. Johnson who lived and died like a Roman in Dagmar Terrace, close to Myddelton Square) but at some point it had overwhelmed him. It had threatened his work, (both as a writer and the university fellowship he had acquired teaching creative English) but also threatened his role as a father and a husband. But typically he had become neither an alcoholic nor a dried-out tea-totalling abstainer, but created his own path which allowed him to conduct long, drawn-out trench warfare with the bottle. It was permitted on weekends, on the holidays that were always taken in Rome (travelling by train, staying in the same old hotel, walking the city) but otherwise it was successfully mastered, and replaced midweek by cigarettes, work and coffee. However I am afraid I found him wonderful company when, just now and then, he slipped off the wagon, for his professional reticence, his note-dropping caution, his steady editorial hand was replaced by a mad hand-waving empowered fluency of conversation, social confidence coupled with free-wheeling indiscretions.

Barry's influence was tangible. I began to try and reach beyond the witty mandarin travel-writers and sieve the world of books for something rarer. He encouraged my interest in micro-history, especially the pioneering works of Gillian Tindall and Rowland Parker, which succeed in giving the people their quiet voice, stilling for once the sophisticated clamour of the gentry, be they landlords, clerics or our great 19th-century novelists. He was also a great champion of the humanity and veracity of Dervla Murphy, the self-willed Irish travel writer whom we would later publish, and was crucial to our range of poetry of place titles, though he refused to take up an editorial role.

One of the keys to our friendship was our differences. The first was a question of age, for I was exactly a generation younger than him, and when we first met I was caught up in a productive period of writing (and being published) that must have reminded him of his own past, before the commissions dried up. The other great difference was class. Barry would gently, but time and time again, correct my assumptions, and remind me of the realities of a normal Londoner. They did not own photograph albums which stretched back six generations (though they might own a single snap of a grandfather in uniform or from a wedding day) ; they did not think that a wall was bare if it was not hung with original art ; they did not think that going to university was in the normal progression of life ; or that every week of your life might be expected to include a number of candle-lit dinner parties. He was never aggressive, but it was very useful to be reminded how many of my assumptions and expectations were embedded in the privilege of my generation and upbringing. And to be gently reminded of the men who had toiled as clerks by day and worked the nights in order to win their education.

But Barry was also mocking of his own ascent into the rarified world of literary London. He remembered with documentary accuracy what an indifferent, if not bored and shirty, student he had been as both boy and young man, only interested in music, films, cigarettes, booze and girls. According to the tale he told me (which may have been entirely fictitious) it was his natural eye for bat and ball that led to being hand-picked for the regimental cricket team during his years of National Service. And it was only then, in the chance company of one passionately literate officer, that he discovered the enchantment of books and verse. Two other men of Barry's generation whom I also got to know at this time, the Irish-American writer John Freely and the photographer Don McCullin, shared this back story. A delicate filament of chance took them out of the working class, through the happenstance of an educational opportunity during their years of national service. I think it was that continued delight in where his life had led him that made him such a determined chronicler, such a diligent diarist. But at other times, I also wondered if words had become almost too important for Barry, how things couldn't exist until they had been properly recorded.

But our differences in age and class, much relished and cherished and commented on by both of us, were surprisingly resolved by tennis. One of Barry's three daughters married a friend of my younger brother, and they had both been on the tennis team of their expensive Scottish boarding school, then patronized by the Royal Family. This odd link tickled us both. It was one of those filaments of inter-connection that the middle classes thrive on (based on the mapping of the Venn diagram like circles of prep school, public school, university, regiment and profession). Another link appeared through the pink uniform of an early-evening ballet class which brought one of my daughters, Molly, and one of his granddaughters, Matilda, together once a week. So I got to know one of Barry's daughters, then by osmosis his whole family through an exchange of birthday tea parties. The Cole family were true natives of our parish, descended through their mother Rita from one of the 19th-century Italian migrants (I think they came from Lucca,) who turned this part of London into a creative little Italy, still complete with its own church, annual parade, Italian foodshops and the genius of Grimaldi, who invented the role, costume and aura of the modern circus clown at the Drury Lane Theatre. Barry (though not of this clan by blood, for he was an Anglo-Saxon born in the south of London) became deeply immersed in the traditions of London's Little Italy, and became their chronicler and occasional poet. I was right impressed.

But there were lines in the sand. We would talk whenever we met, which over any one week could be at Phil's Metropolitan Books on Exmouth Market, at publisher's launch parties, or at any one of our rat-run of café tables, but I don't remember either of us crossing the threshold of each other's door, unless it was to return a parcel of borrowed books or some proofs. It certainly never occurred to either of us that our lone wanderings through the back streets of London would be improved by the company of another person. Nor do I recall that we ever telephoned each other, let alone set a date in which to meet. The proper manner of discourse, which suited both of us, was handwritten notes dropped through each other's letter boxes, photocopies of works in progress or chance conversation.

When I look back over the years, I realise that we must have made some advance arrangements. How else did I meet such friends of his, such as John Wright, an expert on Libya, Chad and the Sahara, and Italian colonial history, with whom Barry had worked with back in his Ministry of Information days? Or Mohammad Ben Madani, that passionate scholar of Moroccan and North African history, who ran both a bookshop, a hospitable table for passing scholars from SOAS, and an academic journal? Was that another Ministry connection? I doubt it, for Mohammad always had a very healthy disrespect for the machinery of state. Or that maverick professor of English literature who is based in Nottingham, who could drink you under the table, play jazz, run a literary publishing house, stay true to the left, create poetry, love Greece, and casually give us a book that we would publish to great acclaim. You couldn't have invented any of these three men, who are united by their independent minds, the active way in which they cherished their freedom, but who are also driven by a passion to understand and a duty to speak their minds, free of cant or the place-seekers' caution. They were all proud of their friendship with Barry Cole, as am I.

Barnaby Rogerson

25. 6. 97

Dear John,

Lovely card you sent from Aegina — simplicity of blue doors, melon-coloured urn and sunbathed pelargoniums — it brightened a rain-sodden English summer day; thank you!

Congratulations on lining up Barry Cole for this cracking good New & Selected from Shoestring! _Inside Outside_ is a lovely, meaty bringing together of delightful poems by a poet who seems to have been able to write mature poetry with a compelling but quiet voice — he never shouts at you, but you listen — all his life. I started to list the poems I particularly liked but there were so many: 'Man Day', 'Nothing to be Observed' — a real beauty, 'Reported Missing,' the wit I found in many places, like about the Minister of the Sea in 'Vanessa'; his ability to summon up forgotten feelings without actually naming them ('Noise after Drinking'); all the poems off from Stely I love, and so many more — 'Odes Against' 'First Person Singular', 'Punctuation' — I could go on & on. It's probably

'Last River Lingular', '&O.', 'Punctuation' – I could go on + on. It's probably fairer to say that the only poems he previously read from Rummy-hole were the Linton's anthology-ised, the 'Haven be Young Bank', and the 'Chadelein', Keatings poem – except one, do you can imagine his surprise – and pleasure. I am to have this 100-page-worth at last a wide variety of moods but always, always presented with a mastery of form and projection of tone I'd have killed for!

So really delightful fine book. Selina Hill's Violet came at about the same time, as a PBS choice, and set me off again gunping the system. Well, I didn't get my choice between the two. You can tell you, Selina again, and she let Rummy-hole know of the enjoyment its poems give me and of my admiration (only) of his deft handling of form – give him my thanks, too.

Best as ever,

Maurice.

HALF-TIME

In memory of Barry, and for Rita, I have chosen part of a novel which has grown (in a good year) at the rate of about a chapter a year from almost the time we first got to know each other. That was fifty years ago, in the Percy Arms, the Coles' next-door pub, sometime in the winter of 1965-6, when Barry, whose self-belief was already astonishing, was poised for a burst of creativity that would result in four books of poetry and five novels in a mere seven or eight years. In 1970, on being appointed Literary Fellow at the University, Barry brought the family up to Durham. They rented a terrace house in Hallgarth Street, just round the corner from our own home in Church Street. We saw a lot of each other in those two years. Rita hated being uprooted from her home territory, and Barry too had little reason to be enamoured of the North-East, having spent a miserable time as a boy evacuee in the Weardale village of Oakenshaw. But in Durham, where the fellowship was a new experiment, Barry made a big impact. His inaugural lecture (on English love poetry, and including readings from his own work) was impressive for its fluency and authority; he gave informal tutorials to aspiring writers, in the process building up friendships that were to last a lifetime; he took his poetry into local schools (Lotte and I had big doubts about its reception in a special school, but Barry returned in triumph to cry: 'They all got it!'); he was a lunchtime regular of the Hotel Victoria, the homely pub midway between our two houses, where he read the paper, made entries in his notebooks, and played vicious games of dominoes with the locals. In all our neighbourhood there was no finer spectacle than the sight of Barry, Rita, Celia, Becky and little Jessica processing into town; after they had greeted you and passed on how it lifted your heart to look back and see those five flowing manes of hair ranging from sunniest blond to dark chocolate brown!

At some point I plucked up the courage to show Barry the first three short (and only) chapters of this novel I had started to write in the intervening years. I met him in the Vic to receive his report, and he was waiting there at the bar with a full pint and my thin folder before him. 'Well, Barry?' He studied the pint, he stroked his wispy beard, he parted the curtains of his hair, and said: 'It's okay, but there's not very much I can say until you write some more.' When I got home I found he had actually read the typescript very closely, but my writer's touchiness had

74

to take a further knock when I saw he had corrected not only my grammar and spelling but my expression and vocabulary. On the other hand, I was elated to find that two paragraphs had earned a little tick from his probing pencil. One of those paragraphs has not survived the rewrites, but I am still very proud of the other.

Barry and Rita loved discovering Rome together; they went back every year, sometimes twice a year. One time, when Barry was recovering from his first treatment for cancer, we met them in Rome and went for a meal together at their favourite spot in the city, their beloved Ristorante Dell'Omo. It is a small family-run trattoria with a few tables and a TV and mamma in the kitchen and dad out front, and aside from its simple ordinariness what Barry and Rita most treasured was the friendship with the family which has grown up over the years. The following pages from that still not quite finished novel are my own tribute to the most humdrum human aspects of Rome. My hero is a local Durham lad who when he wakes on his first morning in the city (having been dumped by his Italian girlfriend in the course of the terrible preceding night) has absolutely no notion where he is. Barry, can I hope for at least one tick?

Half-Time

I surfaced warily, not wanting to meet the memory of some unforgivable crime, until I recalled that guilty feeling is only a sleep device to keep us in the land of dreams. A bad head was the reason for waking in a sweat, and Smoky lodged on my stomach, warm and heavy. During the long quiet of a Sunday morning she loved to steal upstairs to share body heat, patiently riding the waves of my breathing until she heard Mam getting ready to go downstairs to find her some scraps from the fridge and batter the coal fire awake again with a handful of sugar and a clout of the poker. Sunday morning, all the time in the world to sleep off a Saturday night skinful. A bit of a sweat, a bit of a head, and a faithful puss in the wrong place, wrong time… Smothered in blankets, warm in my smells, I rolled on to my side and pulling my knees to my chest sank back down to the point in the dream where I was squatting out of sight behind the big veg rack in the Pattinsons' shop at our road-end. And then, too late, I recalled it was the dream that was worrying.

Humming numbers, head bobbing to the dance of her pen, Mrs P was totting up our bill on the top sheet of the bundle of old newspapers she kept on the counter for parcelling up. So why, when I was invisible, why the uneasy feeling? That tap-tap-tap was only her red biro knocking the side of her specs as she scribbled, so near-sighted her nose practically touched paper too. This was my best chance, with Mrs P always happy when money flowed her way, me too with such a feeling of relief, quietly undoing my fly. Only the buttons were stuck, also her hums and taps had stopped. Her head stayed down but not bobbing anymore, and I could see her nearest ear was thinking Ada's lad's abnormally quiet, as sure as I now knew her wiry grey hair grew through just a few holes in her scalp, like doll's hair. Her shop was like a second skin, forty years she'd lived in it, so she could sense something was up just as though it was her own dress I was fiddling with. Yet all I'm doing is crouching down here for a better squint at what's on offer among the wrinkled parsnips and muddy spuds, grab the leek I want and never mind old Mrs...

'Mucky robber!' That was Major Arthur's no-pocket-money voice, hoping to scare me out of my hidey-hole. 'Cave boy! Muck want to say shame?' What's he doing here, I'm the one Mam sent shopping, not him. I could hear his heavy breath, see the back of his trench coat ashy with dandruff almost close enough to touch, cut in sections by three slats of the rack. Mam's purse was in his hand, her special purse with the brass zip, I must have left it on the counter for anyone to pocket. He knew I was up to no good, he said he had eyes in the back of his head, pulling the zip, thick fingers feeling inside...

On all fours hoping I looked like I'd lost something, like maybe the purse, I squeezed myself right down on my stomach to wriggle under a sagging shelf heavy with red tins oozing a smell of hot soup. I came out under the springs of Mr and Mrs P's double bed next to the stink of a brimming chamber pot, and spied an open door and reached it still struggling to unbutton while I crawled on down a long corridor lined all the way like their shop window with ten-pound sweet jars packed to the lid. Farthing chews, black bullets, soda balls, gobstoppers, dolly mixtures, bull's eyes, jelly babies all colours, I'll wet myself before...

Funny forgetting they had a bit yard out the back. In the open, under the stars again, I slithered down slippery stone steps free at last to – nipping behind stacked crates of fizz and pop – drain all the pain a bladder can contain. It poured and poured, I was over my ankles in no time. Only the pain was the same, I filled as fast as I emptied. In the light from the door stood Mrs P looking to check I was already over the wall. But the major was after my bones, snuffling like a hound on the leash to sniff out the human leak, fuming 'Okay, spawn here!' while I trembled helpless knowing my only hope was to start in earnest, relax, go with the…

No, it's a dream! A dream, a dream, keep saying a dream, only a dream, a hole will open and you can float through. Say it, want it, and your wish comes true… Gripping the root of trouble and joy like a magic wand I soared over the wall into this one and only wonderful world where what happened never happened and never will.

Safe under bedclothes, panic subsiding as I remembered the major was long since dead and burned, I could tell it was bright day outside because the traffic was heavy on Windy Bank, almost as loud as my breath roaring against the sheet like inside a mask.

There were a couple of callers in the kitchen having a bit crack with Mam. Must be coming up to mid-morning, because she had our Sunday dinner going, I could smell onions and a whiff of sage, imagined good roast chicken in the making. I clung to that notion until a clatter like milk bottles kicked over in our entry had me punting my bed round in a 180-degree spin:

'Katie peel ya?'

'Chaos, pet.'

'Our Laura gave her charm.'

The voices somehow belonged with the terrors I'd left behind, but it was fun too, this sensation that my bed was a raft I could turn at will. To and fro we swung between wall and window as at the strokes of a paddle, back and forth between the puzzle of voices. One moment my head was under my dad's brilliant drawing of the 1937 Cup winners, ears tuned to another odd remark drifting up the stairwell, but next time someone spoke ('Our cat's a boy') I could feel myself lying the other way about under the photo of Signalman R. Rowan on the opposite wall, harking to two strangers having the weirdest natter on the pavement under my window.

'Quell any man-painer, eh?'

'Mauve hairdo.'

'Ow, I kissed a fish end!'

'Boo!'

The traffic honked in my brain like Bank Holiday now, and no way round could I make head or tail of their goon talk. Goodness only knows in what state I'd come home, or why ever I'd want to shift my bed. Straightening a leg would fix my position for good and all, according to whether toes met wallpaper or thin air... They pressed the cold end-board of some wooden frame. Nightmare again, in a padded coffin with my heart in a rubber bag, and then I knew the only way to find where I was and why my throat was as sore as when I first woke after having my tonsils out was to stick my head out of the covers and see something real, no matter how bad.

Black night, save for a thin upright L of light, the reverse angle of my bedroom door. That propelled me through the ceiling into Claudia's no-trespassers bed in the attic, pursued by hot terror we'd overslept and by now Mam... God, no, home's a thousand miles away, she's gone for ever, that door she kicked in my face. The warm nozzle of flesh in my fist shrank to nothing as I saw her mouth twist in disgust at her tears then bite into the knot I tied in the kitbag cord, and even with her back turned I could see by the tremble of her neck how hard her teeth were working. Worse, between her gritted teeth she said something I couldn't quite catch, though every sound was still in my head from yesterday. You'll forget this all so quick. Was that it? Too late to know, because she had unbitten the knot and was filling the bag as fast as she could go, and the voices were right behind the door, loud as police.

'O.K.F.I!'

'O.K.H.A!'

I curled in a ball, heart knocking. Just let's get this over quick! Something toppled off the bed, smacked the floor.

'M.O.V.T!'

Light shone red through my lids, someone was breathing very near. I made my own breath as regular as I could, before opening.

Two eyes with irises speckled brown and gold were suspended over mine, so close they looked as big as round mirrors in the ceiling. When they pulled back with a satisfied-sounding sigh I saw a big moustachioed face I first thought belonged in my dream world. He looked down at me, nodding. I nodded too, since now I remembered shaking his hand last night, that hand now holding up a piece of paper. He was in shirtsleeves too, like last night. Then did he not turn away and seem to grieve for TV soldiers?

78

'Good morning,' he said in very distinct English, eyes lowered to the paper.

'Rise and shine!' His son had popped up by his side, dressed in a white shirt and dark trousers as though it was Sunday after all. 'Wakey-wakey!' There was scarcely space for the two of them, and he spoke with some excitement.

'How many hours slipped by you?' Bending an arm for me to read the face of a large wristwatch. 'How many?'

'Ten after twelve,' I read, when I had my head the right way round. 'So?'

The answer was plain to read in their eyes, but my brain was still running too slow, slower than ever when my mouth opened wide of its own accord for a big ear-clicking yawn. Propping myself on one elbow to look more rise-and-shine, I gradually took in that Smoky was a cold hot water bottle, that not just my head ached but also my left knee, that Jesus was watching from the wall, and I was as naked as the day I was born. Yes, so how many hours had I slept in this big creaking mahogany bed with a fancy white embroidered counterpane half on the floor?

'We won Away Cup,' the younger one prompted. 'Remember?'

For the moment all I remembered was how he could arch the tail of an eyebrow. What had hit the floor was one of my hush puppies, the other being still balanced on the edge of the bed beside my pulsing knee. Seeing me eye them he picked them both up and held them out for close inspection before stowing them beside a chair next to the bed. Odd, they looked almost as new as on the demob day I bought them. He liked my surprise.

'Remember now?'

Stacked on the chair was all I possessed that wasn't in a windowless room at the end of a winding corridor on the top floor of a lost hotel. Every item had come in for special treatment. My three-day-old shirt and vest and Y-fronts had been washed and ironed and neatly folded, my Army jumper looked as clean as it would ever get, even my weary jeans seemed to have recovered some of their blue. Atop the pile, on the packet of ten postcards of the Holy City, perched my old woolly grey socks rolled in a ball. Someone had given as much thought to my turn-out as my own mother would have done. I'd have got wrong off her for blind boozing but she'd have done the laundering just the same, though not half as quick. It hurt to swallow, which brought an awful memory.

The son seemed to read my thoughts. 'After,' he said, 'after the accident, and after the streets, you found too many stairs. Sit with me please, Tony. So we sit and speak, remember, maybe one whole hour.'

'After?'

'Why aye, man! After, after –' all the fingers of one hand reached into his mouth to pull out a yard of imaginary tongue - 'after you spewk! Disgusting!' He looked delighted. 'Dad washed you good and proper. And at the end we put you to bed with a nice hot water bottle. You remember now?'

Probably the sudden burning need to urinate explained why nothing he said could jog my memory. The bed shook agonisingly as the two of them, mistaking why I looked away, made a dive for the pile of clothes. Son shoves a hand up one sleeve of the jumper and then spreads his fingers to show the results of some very professional darning at the elbow, in near-matching khaki yarn and all. Dad holds my jeans up by their belt straps against his sturdy stomach for me to admire the knife-edge creases running down each leg. 'Prisoner of war,' he says in that distinct English, under the bushy brown moustache. 'POW Pasquino Pasquale reporting, Sir!' Clicking his heels and lifting his slightly bulging twinkling eyes to meet those of someone considerably taller. 'At your orders, Captain Bulkington!'

At this Antonio hoys the jumper in my lap and starts on a long story about how his father was taken prisoner after the tremendous siege of Tobruk, and after a very bad time in a camp in the desert but good treatment by a doctor in another camp way down in South Africa he finally finished up as batman, a very diverting word, in faraway India for an English officer named Bulkington, a good teacher of English and soon a very good friend, a friend for life unfortunately now dead, whereas in that first bleeding cold winter in London he, Antonio, before moving in with Suzanne always put three hot water bottles in his bed, which by combination reminded him of something also very diverting about a man from Spain similarly named Antonio who shared the same gelid basement with the cook and two other workers from the Portofino and who so much hated getting up in the early morning in that bestial British climate that he convinced the landlady to serve his typical full English breakfast the night before... 'Okay?' he broke off, looking both worried and amused. 'Better when you get a good coffee in there, eh?' forefinger jabbing only inches off my ballooning bladder. 'Or tea? We have a nice big flowery teapot from England. Or coffee the good Italian way, with stacks of hot milk? The WC is…'

I was out of bed already, hopping bare-arsed on my best leg into my snow-white Y-fronts as I headed through the open door, the rest of my gear slung under my arm or round my neck. The bathroom was just across the corridor. Behind me, before I clashed the door, I heard good-natured laughter and the sound of shutters being banged open to let in fresh air. Barefoot on cold floor tiles, spouting like a burst hot-pipe, I stared in grateful wonder at the steaming remains of the past mysterious night of agony tumbling into pelted jostling harmless bubbles. When I lifted my head I imagine the look on my face was not so different to that of the survivor of a pit disaster who hasn't seen normal light and life for days.

The light was broad daylight, brightest in a slender gold sunbeam which sliced through one corner of a high-placed half-open window almost within reach of where I stood. The sky in the window was summer blue, and mirrored in the angled glass was part of the sun-warmed outside of the building, cracked pinkish plasterwork crossed by a brown downpipe. Normal life was this small white-tiled space smelling of soap and fresh paint, with bath and shower protected by a yellow plastic curtain part-reflected in a green-edged mirror screwed above a hand basin. Under the window, just a step away, was a solid wood box topped with pink foam rubber standing about eighteen inches high, the perfect height to give a normal-size person a leg up if he happened to fancy a closer look at how the day was doing. Fixed to the wall near my left elbow, at what would be a seated person's eye level, was a little joke tile with captions in Italian and a picture of what he would be sitting on.

Still tethered to the pan by running rope I edged round it towards the window. Now the pane reflected a red ripple of tiles against the blue, and when I reached up and gave it a little push a line of nappies showed bouncing in the blue with brown arms going among them to add another white flag to the row. Never noticed that before, that the sun can be shining through a pane of glass and it will still act like a mirror.

To my mind, at least in the next couple of minutes, no normal routine could beat sitting in the sun with my pants round my ankles and the extra diversion of trying to make sense of the four lines of writing on the tile. I didn't just read them with my eyes, I repeated them over and over until I felt I had the right rhythm, the true Italian rise and fall.

81

E' GRANDE IL PAPA
E' POTENTE IL RE
MA QUANDO QUI SI SIEDONO
SON TUTTI COME ME

Not easy to render half so tunefully in English, Italian being music to the ears no matter what its drift, all the same I felt I might have it in me to produce a passable equivalent. While working out my version I was put in mind of what a sergeant in the Education Corps, hence a fair linguist, had to say about beginner's difficulties when you first go over the water. We were chugging through flat beet fields in the middle of Holland and the packed troop train was stifling hot and me and Taffy were standing at an open window listening to this much-travelled sergeant-professor telling us how a modicum of patience is all it takes if you want to achieve the seemingly impossible, the rest of the battle being nothing worse than solid hard slog made more tolerable if eased along by an encouraging word or two from someone who has already been through all the hoops. His own words of encouragement included a consoling theory that there are three main phases all go through, dunces and geniuses alike. First comes the thrown-in-the-deep-end phase, when stunned by how simple everyone else seems to find the whole business you feel doomed to remain forever locked in stony silence, too overwhelmed by the weird situation and your own misgivings to imagine you'll ever express yourself, and yet if only you can summon up the patience to sit it out you'll find there's no abiding cause for such gloom and despondency, almost unawares you're slipping into the second phase, the accumulation phase, when even although the overriding sensation may still be that you're only more and more crammed full of outlandish sounds with no actual outcome in sight, all the while deep down inside you're amassing the vital basis for a great breakthrough into the third and final phase, when one fine day you simply seem to wake up and find all your exertions rewarded, with virtually no strain everything is flowing smoothly, there you are babbling away to your heart's content, Private Rowan, positively effusive. Well now, telescoping Sgt Wakelin's three phases into about the same number of minutes and a couple of inspired hunches, I eventually delivered myself of something which I felt ran fairly smoothly, and not even too far off the mark, as I now know.

GREAT IS THE HOLY FATHER
RIGHT POTENT IS HE
BUT MAMMA WHEN HE'S SITTING HERE
HIS TOOTING SOUNDS LIKE ME

Remember it has to rhyme, old Stick-in-the-Mud at St Wilfred's was wont to say, or bang goes all the music. Shakespeare could forget it, but none of you lot'll ever be Shakespeare. I cleaned up, hoisted my pants, and zipped my jeans humming 'Bless Them All,' the old buffer's favourite tune to hum beside the blackboard while he fiddled with his switch and watched us lot write chopped-up sentences for him. When I pressed the plunger something looking like I'd chewed tobacco for a week took a couple of turns round the pan and swam off to find the shortest way to the Tiber.

And now let's have you, Rome!

Stepping up on to the pink-topped box I stuck my head out of the window, and with cool sill-stone digging into my midriff found I was looking down from a good height into a big communal back yard criss-crossed with fresh washing at every level. The cobble setts far below were laid in curving patterns like in the lanes at home, and you could plainly make out their coggly shapes even under a long puddle covering one side of the yard. The washing lines were made of insulated wire all colours of the rainbow, a lot of them loaded with the Monday wash, our own household's too. A loop of apple-green wire ran from an aluminium pulley near my elbow to another cemented in the opposite wall by another window, a reach of thirty or forty feet, and plum in the middle of our line of laundry looking weirdly out of place dangled my khaki parka, like a parachutist come down among telegraph wires. A pair of scruffy pigeons clung to a balcony rail a floor below, pink worm-claws clenching and unclenching on the rusty rail as they sidled to and fro. From the constant narked downward twists of their heads I worked out that they'd been scared up to this height by a tiny tabby I could see trying to claw out something edible from a hole in a black bin bag in one corner of the yard.

That was all the activity to be seen, but there was so much more to hear. The thick house walls were alive with a medley of voices coming and going behind the open windows and narrow iron balconies cluttered with plant pots and broomsticks and even the odd bird cage. Somewhere a doorbell buzzed, and not far off but out of sight a person or a canary set up a contented whistle, which caused me to realise I'd been about to do the same.

For quite a while I lingered there silently savouring the swarm of sounds and the warm smells of many dinners cooking, letting the good sun roast my hair. With one long heavy pang I thought of her at home in the heart of her family, then it quietly lifted along with the last of my headache, like a tight bandage being unwound. Smoky moped days and days for Scratcher, poor dead mutilated thing, but theirs was a simple and trusting friendship. The tabby was very patiently widening the hole in the bag, and meantime there was nothing those two huffy town doves could do but shuffle up and down their short length of rail between big white enamel basins strapped to each end, packed with greenery. Truth to tell, I was beginning to feel a bit like a peckish roof-roosting creature myself, in fact I was just as startled as the birds when a fresh white apple core having made the long trip unnoticed from a great height smacked the cobbles and spun to a halt under the puss's lifted tail.

Twisting my head to see where it came from I saw only a dazzle of sun. Then something moving in the sun, clearer when I shut one eye. It was a big wicker basket bobbing higher and higher above the roof line and underneath it showed the face of a woman with steady forehead and tightened mouth. Bit by bit she rose up full and straight against the glare as her feet reached the top of steps you could hear her climbing, clad in a dress as black as a nun's though shorter. The parapet at that point is no more than a foot high, but she strode fearlessly alongside it a good many paces before swinging down her basket and standing up tall again to stretch a damp double-sheet along a spare wash-line. The way she went about it looked so deft against that solid-seeming blue, she might have been sticking pegs in the sky preparatory to climbing up.

Not long before Claudia broke the comfortable routine of my post-Army life, some wet afternoon alone in the Essoldo in the company of Sophia Loren in a film called *Yesterday, Today and Tomorrow* was I think the first time I got the feeling that Rome might be a good place to live, and earn your keep as well, naturally, seeing you'd need something coming in to pay for a top-floor flat and ten square feet of flowery balcony on which to pass the time of day while in the sunny bed-sit at your back the bonniest lass in the district hums opera to herself while lovingly ironing your silk boxer shorts and blue Alfa Romeo T-shirts and boiling up the spaghetti and mince for dinner, leaving you to solve such knotty problems as why Roman cats seem to favour a windowsill in the shade over a warm tile in the sun, or why multi-coloured insulated wire is so popular for clothes line, and whether or not the lone bold widow on the rooftop knows that each time she bends down to haul up another bed-sheet from her collection the young Signor in the fourth-floor window across the way can see that in fine weather she likes to roll her black nylons below the soft white backs of her knees. Eventually a time will come, I mused, when you've lived so long around the same familiar yard that you'll need nobody to tell you what a person with a hidden reminiscent whistle is busy at, and it'll be no news that Roman pigeons can purr like cats, and you'll know at once the difference between the sound of a tight kitchen drawer being yanked open and a neighbour's little lass's quick squeak of laughter. And better than anything, it will require no feat of imagination to make perfect sense of every chance remark drifting on the air, so unlike that first Monday long ago when you had no Roman dinner times to compare things with and in the end you were so bemused that your head hatched a seemingly unconnected memory of sitting in the bottom of a row-boat in the company of a tin of red worms squeezed between a pair of grey wellies belonging to a big silent man fishing over the side, or long Sunday mornings in barracks when at last nobody shouts and the air is so still that lying in your pit at midday hugging your imaginary woman you can very clearly hear some poor bugger on fatigue filling a bucket from the red fire-point outside the guardroom a good two blocks away over the other side of the parade ground.

That doorbell was buzzing again, and I was starting to imagine a gassing inside when a low grunt drew my eyes to a small second-storey window much like the one I was hanging out of. Down there in the half-dark framed by the open window I spotted a solemn face staring upwards from under massive eyebrows. My first instinct was to duck out of sight, but sensing that his stern gaze had no interest in anything past the window frame I delayed the move long enough to realise he was keeping company with the Pope.

What a day! A blind man in a dungeon would have known it was special. I stepped down whistling 'Bless them All,' reminded by the fresh chemical odour of all that family washing that I could do with a good wash and brush-up myself…

Hugh Shankland

NAMING THE ANIMALS:
NOTES ON AN URBAN NATURALIST

In a famous essay, 'Why look at animals?', John Berger says that when we look at animals today – which we do mainly through artificial images and popular visual entertainments – we feel a sense of loss, knowing that industrialisation has effectively ended a once intimate or 'peasant' relationship between human and non-human, a natural and reciprocal gaze. Pathetically we try to replace that loss with the acquisition of pets. But this may be to underestimate the continuing importance of our sentient companions. They're still here all right, still living with and around us. Berger goes on to say that eye contact between the animals and us has all but disappeared. Even there he may over-state since there are so many different ways of looking, especially in the city.

Throughout his life as a writer Barry Cole looked at animals – quizzically, affectionately, with great concentration. His view was the distanced, often one-way gaze of the urban naturalist. Even when he risked anthropomorphic identification he was either cautious or whimsical. While he wrote plenty of self-regarding mirror pieces, especially early on, his poems about looking at animals are less solipsistic. They offer relationships that can be neither accepted nor rejected, neither sustained nor resolved, a permanently circumstantial state of affairs.

'A Quiet Time Among the Carnivores' from an early book, *Moonsearch*, finds him worrying – not for the last time – about pets and what we make of them.

> Once we come to carnivores we
> Find ourselves in some difficulty,
> First there is the definition,
> The not knowing where to begin,
> The impossibility of order,
> Such as dog, or cat or bear.
>
> Secondly, there is experience
> Of these animals, and the sense
> That only the second and perhaps
> The first would suit the laps
> Of those lovers who prefer an
> Animal love to a human.

> Happily, these are few, but they
> Complicate matters, get in the way.
> What to do with dogs in modern
> Cities, whether to feed the cat on
> Tinned fish or meat to make it play,
> These are the questions of the day.

Suddenly, with one of those leaps into the surreal that he managed so well, the poet is interrupted by 'a large bear' who objects that such worries distract from more important matters. In response to which the poet decides to 'stay with what I knew':

> That is, cats and dogs, for a few
> Of the former have been named by
> Me and others by my family.

Returning to his work he discovers

> that carnivore had bitten
> deep into the page, closed over
> my pen, my arms, my head with fur.
> (*Moonsearch*, pp. 25-6)

On this occasion a shared animality overwhelms tame domestic language.

Nevertheless, we have it on the poet's own authority, in a late poem called 'Punctuation', that when home and alone what he liked above all was to 'watch – an obsession/ this: dogs padding, leaping, Myddelton Square' (*Inside Outside*, p.92). There's vivid evidence of the habit in the poem that follows: 'Freeze Frame, Myddelton Square' dated '*late summer, 1994*'.

> Through plumbago, tobacco plants, morning
> glory, the dogs are being walked: by Eileen
> with her Sheep; the Neat Girl and her Scottie.
> Danny: Killer, Baby Killer; Reading
> Man's brown dog; old Buffalo; the heir to
> Naughty Little. Meaningless names, I know,
> (*Inside*, p. 92).

'Meaningless' perhaps, but through this rueful Adamic reenactment man, woman and dog are permanently 'taped, snapped up, recorded'.

'Was it Beckett (and several others, perhaps including Stevie Smith) who first pointed out dog's anagram?' asks 'Stephen', the would-be novelist in *The Giver* (p. 86). Though both are far from godlike – the point of the anagram, of course – in Barry's view it's usually the case that men are more like dogs than dogs are like men. And not in a good way. When in a poem from *Blood Ties*, entitled 'Man and Dog' (p. 3), a man protests at the female slur that 'men are like dogs', he soon proves it to be true:

> All men, she repeats, as I climb upon
> Her lap, seeking temporary contentment,
> In the manner of their approach are dogs.

The same thought – and presumably the same poem – recurs in the novel *The Search for Rita*. 'Men – they were like dogs, she thought, recalling a poem she had once read. It was the way they approached her' (p. 141). In 'Love me, dog my love' (*The Visitors*, p. 48), love comes like 'a silent growl in an empty room'. Dogs are not to be trusted. A trodden-upon pet may merely yelp but, as his owner points out, 'he'd have your foot for bone if he thought you meant it' (*Joseph Winter's Patronage*, p. 33). Yet despite the small worm-ridden dog that the poet actually wants to kill (*Moonsearch*, p. 10), they are still worth watching. From the black dog who 'holds/ a green ball, wheels and runs as she/ cavorts' (*Inside*, p. 98) to a 'wretched dog, its short legs whirling across the thick grass like mower blades' (*A Run Across the Island*, p. 51).

Ulysses in the Town of Coloured Glass (1968) is something of an anomaly in its treatment of canine prowess. A portrait of the young dog as a psychedelic artist, this trippy sequence belongs to the moment of 'Lucy in the Sky with Diamonds' and 'the girl with kaleidoscope eyes'. We're told that 'Ulysses, a dog, unable to see colour, is fixed with a pair of coloured spectacles'. 'His mind expands', says the gloss, and it certainly does:

> When the butcher's
> Quince-shaded van brakes
> Before the village pond
> The housewives run.

> Green with envy
> See them hurry
> For best-end-of-neck
> For chop and emerald cutlet.
>
> Ulysses, treading
> Sawdust beneath
> His pale-green pads
> Bows for bones of beryl. (p. 37)

He's a surrealist wanderer, is Ulysses, grateful for what he can get – and maybe not a real dog at all. Beneath the skin this hippie dog is clearly a man.

Cats do much better than dogs in the Great Percy Street bestiary, welcomed into the home perhaps for the very reason that they're less easy to accommodate within the human view of things. They often seem antipathetic, and are therefore more interesting. 'On Strega's Several Lives 1970-1984' is a full-scale elegy that commemorates a cat bought in Durham market for ten shillings and later transported to Great Percy Street, 'passing Whittington's cat's memorial/ on Highgate Hill' (*Inside*, p. 86). It's a sometimes funny, sometimes sentimental, sometimes cruelly clear-sighted poem that never slides into any mood for very long as it treats the pain and the power of pet owning. Strega goes hunting, 'skirting alien traffic/ in search of food and – what else – our comfort'. Not that the outside world – this is Islington after all – offers anything like a 'natural' environment: 'Cladding your paws with tar was foolish but/ gentrification was never your style'.

The Giver has a cat called Jesus. He's honoured with this name because 'animals and religion are the main ingredients of a bestseller, which is what this book is meant to be' (p. 37). The book has four shamelessly digressive and ostentatious pages devoted entirely to cats (pp. 123-6) – a long list of quotes from several languages including Montaigne's celebrated quandary, scrupulously reproduced in unmodernised French: 'Quand ie me iove a ma chatte, qui scait si elle passes son temps de moi…'. ['When I am playing with my cat, how do I know she is not playing with me?'] There will, incidentally, be a fittingly playful take on that lasting dilemma in 'Punctuation' when, left on his own, Barry can 'pretend to kick the cat (she makes as if to flinch)' (*Inside Outside*, p. 92), offering the game as mutual, poet and pet equally feigning.

'Stephen' in *The Giver* mentions La Fontaine, Béranger, Gautier and Gay (by-passing Christopher Smart, Charles Baudelaire and, of course, T.S. Eliot who are, perhaps, all too familiar for this aspirant but pretentious novelist). He opts instead for a little-known Italian poet Lorenzo Pignotti (1739 – 1812), author of *The Cat and the Goldfish (Il Gatto e il Pesce Dorato)*, a fable in which a cat who lusts after a beautiful fish with 'rainbow scales and silver sheen' finds, when he tries to eat it, that the uncooked flesh is disgustingly unpalatable. Stephen's claim that his is the first translation into English does indeed seem to be true so the text should probably be added to the bibliography of Barry Cole, poet. The last lines of a clever Augustan pastiche are not only reminiscent of Thomas Gray's 'Ode on the Death of a Favourite Cat', they anticipate the title of Barry's 1997 volume of new and selected poems:

> But still a moral he had to confess
> Although he continued to swear and shout –
> Do not be led astray by a fine dress
> Or estimate the inside by the out.
> (*Giver*, p. 125)

Stephen goes on to quote the first line of a tricky exercise by the excessively obscure poet Henry Harder. This is simply called 'Cats' and it is apparently made up of a hundred lines in Latin, each and every word beginning with the letter C: 'Cattorum canimus certamina clara canumque'. [No translation is supplied though an approximate rendering might be 'Cats canine caterwauling contests chant']. Not surprisingly this feat finally prompts Stephen's literal-minded lodger Patrick to intervene:

> 'What a load of old rubbish,' said Patrick. 'A cat's a cat, and that's all. Jesus doesn't go around thinking like you and me, does he? You ought to have more sense. Cats are cats.'

No doubt – but this doesn't take the matter of animal/ human relations very far. Language demands that animals become other than what they appear to be if they're to enter into the world of the human imagination. Reading great writers who engage with this problem –

Montaigne, Beckett, many, many more – always suggests new ways of thinking about them.

Another Cole favourite, Vladimir Nabokov, encourages us to look again at *Lepidoptera*. From *The Giver*:

> A moth came into my room last night, red and brown, Nabokovian, like a butterfly but for the cigar-butt body. It beat its wings against the two light bulbs. I turned them off, but could hear it flipping in the darkness.
>
> This morning, early, when I put the lights on again, it reappeared from inside the room. I opened the window and door leading to the garden, turned off the lights. The daylight, brighter at that time of day, attracted the moth. (*Giver* p. 40).

Moths love light trustingly, yet humans who can actually control light are just as vulnerable to its deceptions. A poem with an exact title that Nabokov might have appreciated, 'PERIBATODES RHOMBOIDIA' returns us to Barry's early mirror meditations and identifies two indigenous London residents inhabiting the same frame.

> It is late mid-summer's eve. Above
> The pelargoniums, framed by a
> First floor window pane, is a moth. It
> Is not one I know (and there's a face
> I can't identify). My camera's
> Flash whites out, moth, pane, face,
> A print shows the flowers to be blood red
> And the moth to be a White Beauty
> "First identified in London in
> eighteen-thirty one." The face is mine
> (*Ghosts Are People Too*, p. 19)

Respectful identification with insects is disarmingly frequent, perhaps for reasons of scale. In a crowded modern world small things matter. Travelling north by train the poet observes a fellow passenger, an insect:

> Stupid train! To contain such a small
> and scuttling fly, such a slow movement
> towards the hot and overcrowded bar.

This is literal though the poem ends with humble identification:

> I'm only a fly upon a train.
> (*Visitors*, p. 4.)

The wing of a dead wasp, spotted near a grave in St George's Gardens, Camden, makes the poet recall *1 Corinthians 15: 55-56*: 'Death where is thy skin?' (*Inside*, p. 70). Hurrying through the city, 'I speed on… dodge bodies like a wasp between a polity/ of papers' (*Inside*, p. 77). At night 'Fireflies flit behind my window, put place / and time into a long or short perspective (Their lights glimmer intermittently; they live/ as hectic a life as we)' (*Inside*, p. 74). 'Those are ants on the patio – surely/ I know their antecedents?' (*Inside*, p. 89).

There's even a troubling horsefly:

> he does not think
> He is a moth, he cannot think
> Though sensibility's implied.

Struck down by a human hand he takes on uncanny human qualities:

> He falls and leaves behind him
> A pair of legs upon the bed.
> (*Moonsearch*, p. 24)

The passage about the Nabokovian moth in *The Giver* continues:

> And in the afternoon, yesterday, found a spider, two inches ex-legs. Removed by the matchbox method.

Evidence of arachnophilia (a less common human trait, surely, than its phobic opposite?) is frequent. A web can serve as a mnemonic: the 'spiders' skeins ravelling', a memory of the 'bugs and fantasies' that haunted a wartime childhood ('You Can't Go Back', *Inside*, p. 94). It can be a viewfinder ('If I align my view with its centre/ I find I can sight with great precision/ almost any girl passing across the square' ('Spider's Web', *Ghosts are People Too*, p. 17). An arachnid can even be a companion – an eavesdropper like the poet who is himself, perhaps, a relative of Kafka's beetle, surrounded by 'webs, flakes of paint, dust, the occasional spider' (*Moonsearch*, p. 45).

Not all of Barry's animals are Islington residents, domestic or otherwise. A few are quite distant. Confronted by the exotic and unEnglish – a Madagascan 'Fossa' (*Moonsearch, 27*), a marmoset named Sosostris (*Giver*, p. 68) – he sometimes likes to provide the purely scientific terminology (*Cryptoprocta Ferox* and *Callithrix jacchus* respectively). If this seems rather impersonal, let's remember that there was always another side too – a writer incautiously at ease with the weird and wonderful creatures of pure imagination. There's more than one bear in *Moonsearch*. The fourteen-line 'Bear Juggling Flowers', set 'north of Petersburg', asks:

> Did you see the bear, with its doormat
> Back pressed into moss, bark, grass, earth …

'Doormat back' is absolutely right. Barry was never Ted Hughes – no true Londoner, no urban naturalist, would really want to be – and stunning metaphors are rare, but they can startle even so – as here or as with 'a gull's bright hatpin eyes' from a poem in *Blood Ties* (p. 12).

The question about the flower-juggling bear continues:

> And leaves of the ground, the juggling bear
> With furred-thumb turning the air
> Tumbling flowers in a manner we could
> Describe as that of holy pleasure,
> Eyes and paws banging the sun?
> (*Moonsearch*, p. 21)

How can we not see it now, this anonymous solo act deep in the Russian forest? Performed not for our delight but for its own sake – and for that very reason wonderfully visible. 'Dog or cat or bear': although they may escape our nomenclature, as seen through the eyes of the poet they can still live in language. And with Barry Cole they usually did – even those closely observed creatures with their 'meaningless names' who crossed Myddleton Square early in the day.

John Stokes

POSTCARDS IN CODE

After the Bonfire Night fireworks
of *Moonsearch* and *The Search for Rita*
and the sixties buzz I felt
at getting your words into print,
our paths diverged.
Moonscapes of time and space intervened.
Then the odd note, outing, exchange of information,
one welcome collaboration,
and at some forgotten date you began,
like Napoleon, in Noël Coward's "Josephine",
sending postcards, in code, from Rome.
And also, following trips abroad,
meticulous verbal holiday snaps,
gleefully deadpan pages from your journal;
"…A tiny bar where the cassia was guarded
"by a six-month-old baby in a pram…"
"…A dining table laden with fruit, vegetables, bread, meat, wine,
"a half-skinned sheep, and mice fashioned from lemons –
"the usual Last Supper…"

The cryptic texts on your cards would vary:
"ANOTHER OLD CHURCH",
"ONE DAY I'LL GET USED TO THIS PLACE",
"HOW [*beneath a crass caption*] TO BELITTLE AN ARTIST?",
"THE MOUTH OF TRUTH. HA! HA!"
but your message was always the same:
sub specie aeternitatis,
between those who live by words,
solidarity.

Geoffrey Strachan

DOODLING WITH WORDS

i.m. Barry Cole 1936-2014

As if at once inside and outside
his own head. A haze hangs
between the hard-to-pin-down
matter of his mind and the fixed (mostly)
not unlovely outer quotidian

over his half-rememberings
over his ghosts which are real
and his ghostly realities

he is urban, urbane
rude in the right places
perhaps just a *bit* of a goblin, despite denial

he is wary about you, reader
as about his subject, holds both
at arm's length, his lines tracking
the oscillations of his thought
taking off in no obvious direction
trying it this way, that way, turning
back on themselves, doodling
with words

then just when you think you might as well give up
you presto get the whole thing
clean as a whistle, clear as a bell
and you feel as if dipped
in a solving fluid then fished out again

we sit in his room by the twelve panes of glass
talking all sorts while Myddleton Square
below carries on with all sorts (he makes
no excuses for watching the girls down there)

96

oh no, this isn't about missing him
though I wish he were still here
because though the last full-stop has come
each time you broach a poem
you have him back, his voice, the sound of him
full flavour, his ghost, his inside
and outside, his reality.

Hugh Underhill

THERE'S HONEY ON THE MOON TONIGHT

sang Fats in his nineteen-thirties heyday.
Well, so there might have been that night:
on our most often pale-mooned nights
that sounds like wishful thinking.

Instead here in the sun today
the streamlined swifts swing free and easy
cut a dash, play fast and loose, weave
improvisations in blue air, shout a riff
with each high-octane lower-level pass
and then sweep high in aerosonic
chorus or stage a show of pretty fluttering
for slower tempo passages. They take things
in their airy stride the way Fats did, and if
sometimes they're merely clowning
like Fats, to keep us entertained, they're
nonetheless precision high-performance
instruments like Fats's voice and his piano.

This lyric's not by Fats himself, more
goo than nectar-nourishment, but nobody
like Fats could turn a banal song to something
honey-rich, as light and trimly
airborne as those swifts.

'Big in body and in mind' –
so marked his too soon bowing-out
old buddy Andy Razaf – 'a bubbling
bundle of joy, the soul of melody.'

At the Abyssinian Baptist church
his gig was on the organ, but the music that he lusted for
was from the devil's workshop, opined his godly daddy.
Was it then the devil gifted Fats that grace, that pace
that perfect time, that easy swing and syncopation?
If so, god be thanked for such black arts.

Would the moon indeed were spread with honey:
the spacemen might have brought us back
something rich and strange and hinting
ultramundane flavours, unless those mighty
boots of theirs got deep stuck-in for good
by luscious seas of honey.

If I yoke honey, swifts and Fats
too heterogeneously together
why then I cry you mercy, bid you
take your fill of summer skies, watch
the moon's milky crescent rise –
feign it honied if you will –
into a green-tinged dusk as I do now
and taste a track or two of vintage Waller.

Hugh Underhill

BROKEN SONNETS

This sequence of 13 sonnets first appeared in 2008, in a limited edition of fifty copies from Eyelet Books, an offshoot of Shoestring Press. It was originally commissioned by Shirley Toulson who was then running the Happy Dragon Press, but I think that by the time Barry had completed the sequence the press had closed down or was about to do so.

The sequence forms a kind of deliberately incomplete, fragmentary autobiographical sketch, from infancy through childhood to the death of the poet's mother. The frequent ellipses, as well as occasional repeated phrases, are intended to suggest gaps in memory or the difficulty of exact recall, though sometimes they indicate suppression of words/phrases which are too painful to be given expression. One sonnet "I learn to Swim" is a variation on a three stanza, nine-line poem which appears in *Ghosts Are People Too,* where it is succeeded by a ten-line poem in couplets, "My Mother's Death", a title which anticipates that given to the last of the Broken Sonnets.

More than one poet has composed sequences of fourteen sonnets of fourteen lines. That there should be thirteen of these sonnets is intrinsic to the sense of incompletion, of a story not fully told.

I have added explanatory footnotes below each sonnet which seems to need them.

JL

IN THE PRAM

In a sun-heated pram, a smell never
since recollected. A bell ... ...
....
Big hands pulling me away from the ....
... a flapping shawl ... Closing my knell
from or, for what? The sound of green
....
... beneath (I learned later) the ... wheels ...
of an Austin Seven. This would have been
if not ... near the end of nineteen-thirty
-eight or thirty-nine. Some sort of spleen
... slimy greasy heat-retaining ... dirty
.... stick
I have, ever since, been stuck ......

V1S OVER SW!2

The "ones", the old man said, was bollocks ....
farting through the skies like old Nortons ......
You knew where you were ..... Metal balloons
...... they were, so slow and ...... chugging ...
crump! That's what ....
My father marked each detonation on ....
A-Z. I say, that was a bit close ....
he'd say for every other bang ... .
The "twos" was a bugger, said the old man
but my father said they were all the ....
sneaking up Buzz-Bomb Alley, dotting ....
his map Quink marks which bled into ....
It wasn't fair, I said; what have we done
to them? Why can't I ...... shrapnel .... rain.

V1s were flying bombs which the Germans began to send over in the last years of the Second World War. They were soon succeeded by V2s, which flew much faster and were therefore almost impossibly difficult to shoot down. Many civilians were killed by flying bombs during 1944-5. "Norton" was a popular make of motor-bike. "Buzz-Bomb Alley" – the route the flying bombs followed up the Thames before falling mostly on London's East End.

NIGHTINGALE SQUARE RC SCHOOL (1)

I was led into the playground by my
mother. Someone said, go to the end, why
the line? There were five of them but which was
the end? ... .
I walked beyond the last child until I
came upon a wooden fence. "That will do,"
said a teacher ....
I tried to make sense, make out why every
other child seemed to have a place where they
could stand, inviolable, untouchable,
serene – and taller than I at four ...ble
a half. ....
trodden plants (what plants?) ... My very first day
at school; my first milk, my first spoon of malt.

*Nightingale Square, in Balham, SW London, was where, after returning from
evacuation, Barry Cole lived post-war with his parents and siblings.*

NIGHTINGALE SQUARE RC SCHOOL (2)

The church by the school was for Catholics
where girls covered their heads and where I and my
sister had to stand outside because we
were C of E, or so our father ....
.... we once had had a Reverend Uncle up
the road at the Church of the Ascension,
Balham Hill, was it? (anyone .... tics.)
Anyone ..... Remember? The plaque on
the desk; the way he made, re.....ion –
he was there from nineteen-twenty-eight to
nineteen-thirty-two. So nothing. What I
resented was that I couldn't follow
my first love through the door .... How
it could have been .... lie

NIGHTINGALE SQUARE RC SCHOOL (3)

At eleven I fell in love with Jane
Lumiere, her hair lit by candles at an
altar I was told to keep …. …. ….
(Are you still there, Jane, at sixty-seven?.
An angel from a church I could not ….
I bit my upper arm to attract her
attention, but it …. … ….. … ….. leap.
Nothing worked, either at school or in was
it Oakmead Road … … Outside, as
a smoggy night fell across our eyes …
and went home with a sadness heavy as
…. ….. .. any commonplace fog or dark
and the odd fumble …. ….. .. ….. park,
and then the inevitable …… …

NIGHTINGALE SQUARE RC SCHOOL (4)

A gang of four, five, six, armed with bikes. Fit,
wristy, eleven, hurtling around our
genteel square, frightening the pre-war bit
of a society shattered by a war
we didn't understand …. outside……
by the shrapnel collected in those tins
of milk our mother pressed into the twins.
Outside number, five, eleven, forty –
outside the church, the school … …. …
mocking the priest, the teacher, the parents
……. our own directions tight in our …..
unknown. Our bicycles in the gutter,
mimicking the world's turning …. …. …
Asking what will there be for Christmas Day.

SCHOOL DINNERS, CIRCA WINTER 1946-7

Lunch, actually, said my father ... .
Meat and two veg – none of which I would eat.
The flesh smelt of bomb-site drains, green things
... air pie and bug sauce and frogs' spawn ...
Milk and malt; orange juice ... oil of cod's
liver ..... allowed out to slide .... on or off
a playground iced as if forever .... heat.
Miss, Miss! What's a balaclava helmet?
And hands warmed up less by food than snow ...
and yet gloved hands froze.
    What was you dinner like? said my mother
.... did you get enough? Are you hungry? .....
would you like a piece of bread and dripping?
Condensed milk? I wouldn't mind a slide .....

The winter of 1946-7 was one of exceptional and long-lasting cold, during which many children, boys especially, wore woollen balaclavas – close-fitting hoods – pulled over their heads to ward off the worst of the cold. Playgrounds became ice-rinks with long slides made from the impacted, frozen snow; snowball fights were commonplace and sometimes dangerous. Despite poor food – "frogs spawn" is what children called the tapioca puddings served up at school dinners – the Labour Government provided all school children with milk and daily spoonsful of extract of malt (delicious) cod-liver oil (thick -white, fatty, and revolting) and concentrated orange juice.

MORGAN

Rayleigh, Essex. My father bought a three-
wheel car. You could drive home with me, he said
but there is a strong smell of petrol ...
The seller walked me back, bought me twelve .....
for a penny ....
Striving to explain (striving?) my feelings
to my .... and sister, I cried out
....
What ....
the smell of petrol, the bucket seats, the
hood ... smell of wet tweed and dank hair
... the dry, choking taste of the wafers .....
and I'll never forget, ever forget ... .
forget ...., forget...., forget ... ... hate.

The Morgan was a sports car with a single front wheel fixed under its tapering bonnet. Popular in the 1930s, the model was discontinued at the outbreak of war. The one mentioned here must have been bought second-hand. In the immediate post-war years petrol for domestic use was severely rationed and had to be dyed a certain colour to distinguish it from petrol licensed for sale for commercial or other purposes. The dye brought with it a strong smell. Anyone discovered using petrol to which they were not entitled might end up serving time in prison. The rich and the well-connected were not exempt. Sweets were also rationed — and difficult to come by — so whatever was bought twelve for a penny would in all likelihood have been the "wafers" — probably made of flour and water.

I LEARN TO SWIM

One day .... a ... late .... (was it?) ..... 's morning
he said, at the Tooting Bec baths, this is the
deep end. I looked at its green depths, a wobbly wave
distorting the white tiles ... And ... .f, toes
curling as my legs straightened and ... water ...
my ... And this, said my father, is the shallow ... (was there
scorn in his voice?) end. It, too, was green, but, close
up it, too, was green, ..., ...
Of course I jumped/leapt/dived into the wet and ....
my life. ....., .. He ..., listen to me, keep your arms
together, and ... . tight ......, that way you .....
fail. Do you know what I mean? This was the first
time we understood each other, I think, and,
as I dived/leapt. Jumped, I swam ... .

SANDHAM AND GOVER

"You're a bit small, but you've got big hands .. ..
Mr James, look at the spin on that compo!"
And the ball span right to left, almost ....
A hat-trick in the only sport ... so far ..... then
to order. Leave school ... So to work ..... Bring home
your mother ... Stop this cricket! It's not worth the ...
And your bat's rotted ... excess of linseed oil ... Don't
you know ...? No time, no money, no interest, no
future ... What about the Wandle Seconds, the
Bec Thirds? (Done it, done it, done it, why weren't
you watching me?) A couple of years later,
in an airman's cap, I bashed out a fifty,
and then .... thirty.
And was offered three pounds a week to join ....

*Andrew Sandham (1890-1982) and Alf Gover (1908-1990) were well-known
Surrey cricketers, both of whom played in several Test Matches. Sandham was an
opening batsman, while the right-arm Gover was one of the best fast bowlers of his
age. "Compo" balls, unyieldingly hard, were made of compressed cork and regularly
used in playground or street cricket, because they withstood concrete or asphalt
surfaces, though bits would be gouged out by a kerb stone or by the ball's contact
with brick, and this provided extra purchase for anyone wanting to spin the ball.
A leg-break bowler spins the ball from right to left, which Gover certainly didn't
do. Cricket bats were steeped in linseed oil before use, though I've never heard of
one rotted by too much oil. "and then .... for thirty" – "and then took
four/five/nine for thirty"? Hmmm.*

OLIVE POUPART, NEE RYDER

Haunted by my mother's step-sister because:
she took care of me, sixteen to five ....
Held me when ... who? Her father? Her brother .....
screamed and who let me lie supine upon her
breasts and cleaned up my sick. And who looked ...
like Lana Turner as far as I can
remember and sang like, was it, Jo Stafford?
She'd now be eighty-three, and I'm now nearing
Seventy. .... all this ..... the slipping off of
(of) her nightdress, my waking up and ....
a drink and she, ..., ... And then, back in bed turning
to me and saying ... better keep quiet about this it's
not .... my sister (she said "sister") should know
about, like my new dad, who played about like ...

THE COFFEE CABIN, STREATHAM HIGH STREET

When? Nineteen-fifty-seven? Gaggia … ………
Another common (ha!) ground … Twirly frocks
and lipstick applied after leaving home ….
posing and posturing and talking loudly (and that
was just the boys.) *Noli me tangere* but …
Christ forgotten … …….. Saw her home to
the door, a buckled oak …. Front garden phlox ….
Meet again, same place, same coffee, same ……..
Same Saturday, same Sunday …. her new
man came along (jazz on the juke box) and Ella
or Helas, my attraction retracted – ………
destroyed. Or so she thought, but I fought ….
and got her and all her bits and pieces
back enough to say, it's over, over, over ….

MY MOTHER'S DEATH

What I remember is a neighbour saying
that she died on her kitchen floor. And that she
had looked old. That was OK, we'll all do
that. Then she said that her wig had fallen off
and landed before the sink. What was I
supposed to say? … … … and … … .
laughed a year later when, you yourself …., a
died, your wooden leg, which you asked me to put
… … ….. the table where *he* always sat (at least
while I was there, a-drinking and a-dribbling
alongside his old cane chair.) And how you asked
to look through his stamp collection, begun …..
the First World War … stuck down with ……. glue
which killed … … .. … .. ever loved.

*"his old cane chair". An allusion to "Old Rockin' Chair," a song by Hoagy
Carmichael, composed in the 1930s and much played and sung by jazz bands in
the UK during the 1950s. There are two versions of the song performed as a duet
by Louis Armstrong and Jack Teagarden, both of them wonderful.*

The following poem – or notes for a poem – was found among Barry's papers after his death. It was probably written in February, 2014.

Most of my life I have
Tried to avoid
Being late.
"You're too early" was an
Unwanted compliment, but
Served me well.
Recently, like a rattle of
Bones, *Late* has begun to
Intrude into my view of
Say, the next year or two.

CHECK-LIST OF BARRY COLE'S WRITINGS

Poetry

a) Books

Moonsearch, Methuen, 1968

The Visitors, Methuen, 1970

Vanessa in the City, Trigram Press, 1971

Pathetic Fallacies, Methuen, 1973

Inside Outside: New and Selected Poems, Shoestring Press, 1997

Ghosts Are People Too, Shoestring Press, 2003.

b) Pamphlets etc

Blood Ties, Turret Books, 1967

Ulysses in the Town of Coloured Glass, illustrations devised by Edward Lucie Smith, and the frontispiece, designed, engraved and printed from original linocut blocks by Stanislaw Gliwa, Turret Books, 1968

Dedications, The Byron Press, 1974

The Rehousing of Scaffardi, Keepsake Poem 17, Keepsake Press, 1974

Words Broadsheet Twenty-Nine: Poems by Barry Cole, Frank Lissauer, Robert Hill, Words Press, 1976

Broken Sonnets, Eyelet Books, an imprint of Shoestring Press, 2011

c) Poems in Anthologies (selected)

Children of Albion, ed. Michael Horovitz, Penguin Books, 1969

English Poetry Since 1945, ed. Edward Lucie Smith, Penguin Books, 1972

The Oxford Book of Twentieth Century English Verse, chosen by Philip Larkin, OUP, 1973

Continuities: Poems by Byron Press Poets, The Byron Press, 1978

There is a recording of Barry Cole, made by the British Council in November 1967, in which he reads thirteen of his poems and talks about his work.

Prose Fiction

a) Novels

A Run Across the Island, Methuen, 1968. (paperback edn., 1969)

Joseph Winters' Patronage, Methuen, 1969. (Reprinted by Shoestring Press, 2008)

The Search for Rita, Methuen, 1970

The Giver, Methuen, 1971

b) Contributions, including fiction and memoirs, to books by various hands

Evacuees, ed. B. S. Johnson, Gollancz, 1968

London Consequences, ed. Margaret Drabble & B. S. Johnson, London Arts Association, 1972

You Always Remember the First Time, eds. Michael Bakewell, Giles Gordon, & B. S. Johnson, Quartet, 1975

CONTRIBUTORS

Michael Bartholomew-Biggs is poetry editor of the on-line magazine *London Grip* and a co-organiser of the reading series Poetry in the Crypt. His latest publications are *Fred & Blossom* (Shoestring, 2013) and *Pictures from a Postponed Exhibition*, a collaboration with artist David Walsh, (Lapwing, 2014).

David Belbin is the author of many novels, including *The Pretender and The Great Deception*. Since 1989, his short stories have appeared in many magazines, most frequently *Ambit*, and anthologies including *Best Short Stories Of The Year* (Heinemann) and *Overheard: Stories To Read Aloud* (Salt). Shoestring will publish a collection of them in 2016.

Alan Brownjohn's most recent books of poems are *The Saner Places* (2011), a comprehensive selection from twelve earlier volumes, and his latest individual collection *A Bottle, and Other Poems* (2015). His fifth novel, *Windows on the Moon*, appeared in 2009.

David Buckman has been a journalist, author and broadcaster for 50 years, mainly as a freelance, latterly specializing in modern British art. He has contributed to numerous publications, including artists' obituaries for The Independent, The Guardian and The Telegraph. Among his books are the dictionary Artists in Britain since 1945; From Bow to Biennale: Artists of the East London Group; and, most recently, Lancelot Ribeiro – An Artist in India and Europe.

Malcolm Carson was born in Cleethorpes, Lincolnshire. He moved to Belfast with his family before returning to Lincolnshire, becoming an auctioneer and then a farm labourer. He studied English at Nottingham University, and then taught in colleges and universities. He now lives in Carlisle, Cumbria with his wife and three sons. He has had two full collections, *Breccia* in 2006 and *Rangi Changi and other poems* in 2011, and a pamphlet, *Cleethorpes Comes to Paris* in 2014, all from Shoestring Press.

Martin Dodsworth is Emeritus Professor of English, Royal Holloway, University of London.

Steve Hawes produced sport, arts features, and drama for Granada Television from the mid 1970s until 1990, when he moved to Paris to produce Maigret for French television, later writing several episodes in the series – which ran until 2005. In between times he was head of Performing Arts and professor of Drama at Winchester University. He wrote four stage plays for director Paul Chamberlain at the Haymarket, Basingstoke, 2006-2013. His adaptation of Dmitri Verhulst's *Problemski Hotel*, dir. Manu Riche, appears in cinemas in 2016.

Maurice Hindle is an independent writer and scholar. Among his publications are *Shakespeare on Film* (2015), Penguin Classic editions of Mary Shelley's *Frankenstein* (2003) and Bram Stoker's *Dracula* (2003), and (as editor) *The Guide to Shakespearean London Theatres* (2013). His scholarly editions include William Godwin's last novel, *Deloraine* (1992), and Daniel Defoe's *Col. Jacque* (2009). His latest writing project is *Singing His Heart and Speaking His Mind: The Songworld of John Lennon* (in progress). (www.mauricehindle.com)

Nancy Mattson moved from the Canadian prairies to London in 1990. Her third full poetry collection is *Finns and Amazons* (Arrowhead Press, 2012). She co-organises Poetry in the Crypt in Islington, north London.

J.S. McClelland, a former lecturer in Politics at the University of Nottingham, is the author of *The Crowd and the Mob*, and the monumental *A History of Western Political Thought*. He still lives in Beeston.

Paul McLoughlin's most recent collection of poetry is *The Road to Murreigh* (Shoestring Press, 2010). He edited and provided an introduction for *Brian Jones: New & Selected Poems* (Shoestring Press, 2013). He has been known to play jazz saxophones and flute to anyone who'll listen, and occasionally for those who pay.

Tom Paulin, distinguished poet and critic, was a lecturer in the English Department at the University of Nottingham before moving to Oxford in the late 1980s. He met Barry on the many occasions when Barry came to Beeston.

Barnaby Rogerson runs Eland Publishing from the street market that lies three blocks south of Barry Cole's home. It is now the home to over a hundred classic titles of travel and spirit of place books, www.travelbooks.co.uk. For other publishers Barnaby has written a biography of the Prophet Muhammad, an account of the first four caliphs, a history of North Africa and the story of the last crusade, 1415-1578, as well as guide books and editing various anthologies. (www.barnabyrogerson.com)

Maurice Rutherford's *And Saturday is Christmas: New & Selected Poems* (Shoestring Press, 2011) has just been re-issued.

Hugh Shankland headed Italian Studies at the University of Durham between 1966 and 1999. He has written on Italian literature and culture and published a number of literary translations. His most recent books are *Rome Tales* (OUP, 2011) and *Out of Italy: The Story of Italians in North East England* (Troubador, 2014).

John Stokes is Emeritus Professor of Modern British Literature at King's College London and Honorary Professor of English and Drama at the University of Nottingham. His books include *The French Actress and her English Audience* (CUP, 2005) and, edited with Mark W. Turner, two volumes of Oscar Wilde's journalism (OUP, 2013).

Geoffrey Strachan worked as an editor, between 1961 and 1995, in the fields of drama, fiction, poetry and humour at Methuen, where he published a number of Barry Cole's novels and volumes of verse. Over the past fifty years he has translated classic and modern fiction, history and biography as well as verse and stories for children. He has been awarded both the Scott Moncrieff and Schlegel-Tieck prizes for translation. He is the English translator of all Andrei Makine's novels, most recently, *A Woman Loved* (2015).

Hugh Underhill has published five collections of poetry, the most recent of which is *The Shape of Days* from Shoestring Press, as well as a collection of stories *The War is Over* (also from Shoestring). He has also published books of criticism and many critical articles. He edits *The Robert Bloomfield Society Newsletter.*

A FESTSCHRIFT FOR BARRY COLE

Drawing of Barry Cole by Pauline Lucas